Regrets
Only

Gwen Andrews Mystery #5

Lumina...
Gwen on
Nantucket!

Debi
5-28-24

by Debi Graham-Leard

D1593002

Riverhaven

Books

Regrets Only is a work of fiction.
Any similarity regarding names, characters,
or incidents is entirely coincidental.

Copyright© 2023 by Debi Graham-Leard

Published in the United States by Riverhaven Books,
Massachusetts.

Paperback ISBN: 978-1-951854-36-2

Printed in the United States of America
by Country Press, Lakeville, Massachusetts

Front Cover Photo: author Debi Graham-Leard

Back cover author photo: Ria MacKenzie

Edited by Riverhaven Books
Designed by Stephanie Lynn Blackman
Whitman, MA

Previous Novels
by Debi Graham-Leard

The Uninvited Guest
Introducing Gwen Andrews
2015

Where There's Smoke, There's Trouble
Gwen Andrews Mystery #2
2017

Bed, Breakfast, & Blackmail
Gwen Andrews Mystery #3
2019

Wedding Interrupted
Gwen Andrews Mystery #4
2020

The Life She Left Behind
a contemporary novel
2021

Acknowledgements

I want to thank the following people for sharing their expertise during the development of *Regrets Only.*

Det. Jesse Winters … Norton, MA, Police Department, and former Nantucket officer.

Debbie Ahern… source for Nantucket hauntings.

Nancy Robbins Federici… Nantucket traveler.

Lt. Angus MacVicar… Nantucket Police Department.

Rick Blaire, Sconset Bluff Walk guide.

Pamela Loewy… treasured reviewer.

Jerri Graham Burket… my sister who provides a writing prompt each and every morning.

and

Vinnie Leard… my sweetheart of a husband, who never discourages my time spent writing.

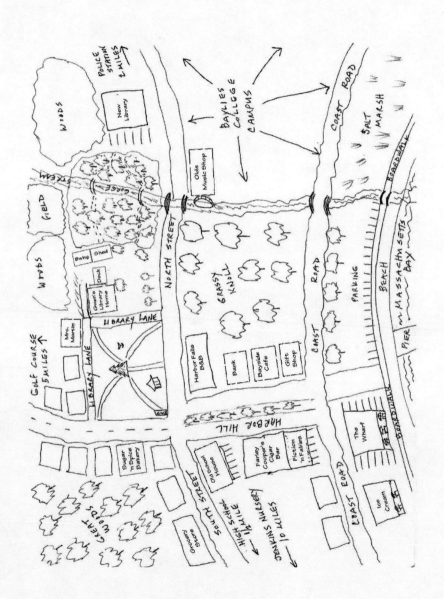

Not All Invitations Bring
the Fun They Promise

Chapter One

… early morning, Thursday, late October

After switching on her coffee maker, Gwen Andrews gazed through the kitchen window to watch the sun easing above the horizon, bathing her back garden in gold-tinged light. Though widowed and retired from her professorship at the local college, she remained an early riser.

When the coffee maker beeped, she reached for the carafe. At the same instant, her cell phone vibrated against her hip. Pulling it from her jeans with her free hand, she lost her grip on the carafe, and it crashed to the unforgiving tile floor.

Gwen froze to avoid stepping on the shards as she wrestled the still-vibrating phone from her pocket and smiled at the caller ID... her elder sister, who lived in the Berkshires, far enough from Gwen's library home on the Massachusetts coast that they didn't pester each other, close enough for several visits each year.

Gwen pressed the green icon. "Tess, what's wrong?"

"Nothing's wrong. I knew you'd be out of bed by now, and I couldn't wait any longer to ask you a question."

"Go ahead. I'm listening."

"Do you have any plans for this weekend?"

Gwen glanced at her wall calendar. "A young piano student Saturday morning. We can work around him if you're driving over for a weekend visit."

"You're partially right."

Gwen grinned. "Enough teasing. What are you up to?"

"To quote a notorious movie trilogy... *I'm gonna make you an offer you can't refuse.*"

Amused, Gwen joined Tess's game. "And the offer is?..."

"An all-girls Halloween party on Nantucket!"

"Sounds like fun. And I'm due for a road trip. Who's hosting the party?"

"Do you remember my college roommate Julie?"

"Of course. You've stayed in touch all these years?"

"Birthday and Christmas cards, an occasional phone chat. But we haven't laid eyes on each other in decades."

"And she's living on Nantucket?"

"Yep. After she divorced her second husband this past spring, Julie bought a cottage on the island and has been renovating all summer. Her Halloween party is doubling as her housewarming. Oh, and we're supposed to bring costumes. Are you game, Sis?"

Gwen hesitated. "Before I commit, I'll see if I can cancel

my Saturday student without upsetting his mom. Too early to call them right now. How about I let you know later?"

"Okay, but I'm going with or without you," Tess warned in her practiced big sister tone.

"As you should."

Gwen's doorbell chimed. "Someone's here."

"You go answer your door, and I'll start packing."

Tiptoeing around the glass shards while tucking her phone back in her back pocket, Gwen strode to the living room window to see a bright red Corvette gleaming at the curb. Glancing left toward her front steps, she recognized the distinctive white hair of Detective Benjamin Snowcrest, her friend and sometimes sleuthing partner. He crossed his arms against the autumn chill then shifted his weight to lean against the iron railing.

Hurrying to her foyer, Gwen paused at the antique mirror and fingered her ash brown layers until she deemed herself presentable.

Pulling open the heavy oak door, she smiled at him. "Good morning, Ben. Did we have plans I forgot?"

He pushed himself upright. "Nope, no plans. Hope you don't mind me stopping by with no warning."

"Not at all. I'm always glad to see you." She held the door wide for him to enter. "I'd offer you a cup of coffee, but I just now dropped the carafe and it shattered."

Ben's expression contrite, he asked, "My fault for ringing your doorbell?"

"No, no. My sister's earlier call startled me."

"Glad it wasn't me. My bad luck, though – I do love your coffee," Ben said. "How about I help you clean up the mess?"

"I accept your offer… thanks."

They soon pitched soaked paper towels into the trash basket, shattered glass plus plastic into the recycle bin.

"Thanks, Ben. If you don't have to rush off, why don't you light the kindling I arranged earlier? I can heat some cider, and we'll catch up."

"How can I refuse?"

After warming the cider and adding a cinnamon stick to each mug, Gwen took a seat at one end of her leather sofa, watching Ben strike a match to the crumpled newspaper in the double-sided fireplace.

Her focus strayed to the nearby recliner, where her husband Parker's ghost had stretched out in his favorite chair several years earlier. He'd appeared that day with no warning, easing Gwen from her grieving of his premature death. Each of his subsequent visits was more comforting than the last. More recently, when she'd nearly died herself, he'd pushed her back into life and promised to be waiting for her on the other side when her time came.

Glancing at Ben now, Gwen couldn't help but compare the two men. One living, the other a ghost. Ben had hinted he wouldn't object to a deeper commitment with her. But did Gwen dare risk her link to Parker's spirit by allowing her fondness for Ben to edge beyond friendship?

Any believer in the paranormal would understand how this triangle complicated Gwen's earthly life. Ben, a flesh-and blood man, could provide physical comfort. Parker's ghostly capabilities were limited, not to mention his inconsistent visits.

Gwen's challenge constantly tormented her. Was she obligated to choose one over the other? Or could she enjoy both? Ben while she lived, and Parker after she passed.

Did anyone exist who could answer that question?

When Ben settled two cushions away, Gwen's internal debate came to an abrupt halt. "Haven't seen much of you lately. What's been going on?"

Shifting to face her, Ben scowled. "Chief Brown keeps forgetting I'm retired and constantly requests my assistance. I didn't mind bridging the gap at first, but as soon as I've closed one case, he yanks me into another."

Gwen tucked one bare foot beneath her. "He hasn't replaced you yet?"

"No, he hasn't. He could easily promote a squad member or recruit a detective from the regional task force, but he's taking his sweet time to do it."

"Can't you refuse his requests?"

After picking up his mug and taking a sip, Ben shook his head. "The chief and I go back a lot of years. I'd hate to lose his friendship by turning him down. I'm sorry, Gwen. I'd expected to be spending *more* time with you, not *less*."

"I completely understand. No need to apologize." Turning her attention to the flames licking at the seasoned logs, Gwen held her mug with both hands, allowing the warmth to permeate her fingers. Though she empathized with Ben's frustration, she had no other solutions to offer.

Ben interrupted her trance. "How about dinner Saturday?"

"Sorry, my weekend is a little up in the air at the moment. My sister invited me to a party."

"Are you going?"

"If I'm able to cancel a Saturday piano lesson."

"What does your Sunday look like?"

"If I go to the party, I won't be back until late Sunday."

"Again, my bad luck."

"Why is that?"

"I stopped over to invite you to a concert at Baylies College on Sunday afternoon."

"I'd love to go with you if I'm not on Nantucket with Tess."

Ben's eyes widened. "Nantucket?"

"Yes. Did you already buy the concert tickets?"

"I did. I should have invited you days ago. Then you could have told Tess you had plans." His cell buzzed, interrupting their conversation.

"Give me a sec to check this text." As he read it, his expression darkened. "The chief. No surprise. He wants to see me in his office. I need to get going."

Gwen's eyes widened as Ben finished the rest of his cider so quickly he could have won a chugging contest. She rose to walk through the foyer, tugged her oak door inward, and stood aside to let Ben exit.

Instead of sliding past her, Ben paused. "If Saturday is a no-go, how about dinner tonight?"

"Nice idea, but if I take the ferry with Tess tomorrow morning, she'll be arriving here later today."

"Then I'll treat you both."

"Very generous. I'll let you know our plans."

"Just in case, I'll make a reservation at The Wharf and pick you both up around six."

When he leaned toward Gwen, his intention to kiss her obvious, Gwen shifted her face to one side, his lips instead grazing her cheek.

Without commenting on her evasion, he straightened. "I haven't traveled to Nantucket for years. I think I'm jealous. See you later… with or without your sister."

Gwen waved as Ben's Corvette zoomed around the village green, red-tinged leaves skittering in his wake.

Chapter Two

… early morning, Thursday

Closing the door, Gwen paused in her foyer and reached for the treasured photo of her departed husband Parker. Her arm had circled his waist as they strolled the sands of Duxbury Beach. She recalled seagulls winging overhead as quiet waves lapped at the shoreline.

The following week, he'd been struck by lightning, passing away days later with no chance to say goodbye.

She'd mourned Parker desperately until the astonishing afternoon that his ghost materialized in his recliner. Accepting his paranormal state, Gwen anticipated his sporadic visits, mostly when she was upset.

Switching her thoughts to Ben Snowcrest, she mulled over her history with the detective.

She'd first encountered him during his investigation of a murder down near the harbor. When her friend Liz was deemed the prime suspect, Gwen ignored the detective's warning to stay out of his police business and set her mind to proving Liz innocent.

When Gwen uncovered the real criminal, she'd sensed an increased respect from the white-haired detective. He'd enlisted her to work behind-the-scenes on other cases and their relationship blossomed into a warm friendship. They rode along the back roads of New England, enjoyed seashore dinners, and once an evening of dancing. She thoroughly enjoyed Ben's wit and companionship.

That past June, he'd been out of town on police business when she'd nearly died at the hands of a murderer she'd cornered. When Ben heard about it, he kissed her, and she'd unthinkingly responded.

No wonder Ben now hoped for more than friendship.

But he wasn't aware that she'd almost died a second time, later on that same June day.

After the stress of catching the murderer, she'd fainted in Parker's recliner. Not surprisingly, his spirit appeared to her. She'd reached out, prepared to walk beside him into the afterlife. But Parker pushed her back toward her body, saying, '*Not your time, sweetheart. I'll be waiting for you.*'

Understandably, that life-altering event had solidified Gwen's devotion to her beloved husband.

Now, she had to tell Ben about Parker's promise, the reason for her recent coolness. Ben's hurt expression just now after she turned her cheek to avoid his parting kiss filled her with unavoidable regret. But he needed to understand that she wasn't willing to risk her paranormal connection to Parker by embarking on an intimate relationship with Ben… or any other living man, for that matter.

Her heart ached that she might lose Ben's friendship. At her age, genuine friends were hard to find.

She speculated that her triangle with Parker's ghost and the human Ben was unique and didn't happen to most widows.

Gwen's cell phone vibrated, providing a bittersweet distraction from her dilemma. Was Ben calling to say he wouldn't be available for dinner with her and Tess?

Placing Parker's framed photo gently on the foyer table, Gwen lifted her phone to check the caller ID. Not Ben.

Chapter Three

… mid-morning, Thursday

Gwen pressed the green icon to take the call.

"Mrs. Andrews, this is Mrs. Hardy. I hope I'm not calling too early."

The parents of Gwen's music students rarely called. Was there an issue with her child's piano lesson?

Gwen answered the question. "Not too early at all."

"Would you mind awfully if I cancel my son's lesson on Saturday morning?"

If only all of Gwen's challenges could be resolved so easily. "That's not a problem, Mrs. Hardy."

"Oh, thank you. I'll drop him off the following week. Thanks for understanding. Goodbye."

With Saturday's commitment off her plate, Gwen dialed her sister. "I'm free to go with you, Tess. But aren't the lodging places on Nantucket closed by now?"

"Probably," Tess answered, "but we'll be staying at Julie's cottage the entire weekend, along with an unidentified third person. The other party guests live on the island. We'll need to take the fast ferry tomorrow morning."

"In that case, you should drive over here today."

Tess laughed. "I've already packed my car."

"Smarty pants. Let's shop for costumes this afternoon."

Ending the phone call a minute later, Gwen opened her laptop on the kitchen island counter and searched for costume shops. If nothing suited them at the local party store, they could explore the Halloween outlet one town over.

Next, Gwen clicked into the Nantucket weather forecast. Seasonably cool with a chance of a shower.

Her buzzing cell phone began to dance across the granite surface, and she grabbed it before it tumbled over the edge, grinning when she discovered the caller.

"Hello, Jenna. What can I do for my sort-of granddaughter?"

Jenna Jenkins laughed. "Just answer one small question, my sort-of grandmother."

They'd been using these faux titles since Gwen invited Jenna to stay in the guestroom while pursuing her music degree at nearby Baylies College.

"What's your question?" Gwen prompted.

Jenna's voice filled with excitement. "A classmate invited me and a few others to Vermont for the weekend. Before I say yes, will that cause you any problems?"

"Not me. Sounds like a pleasant break from your studies." Gwen hesitated, considering the rest of her response. "Actually, Tess invited me to Nantucket this weekend."

"Are you taking Amber with you?"

"No. I'll ask Liz to stop by after she closes her bookshop to feed and check on our brat cat."

As if eavesdropping, the cat strolled down the open staircase like a homecoming queen, pausing on the third tread, a suspicious gleam in her eyes.

"If you're sure Liz can do it, I'll walk home between classes to pack. We're leaving right after our last lecture. What's the schedule for you and Tess?"

"She'll arrive here around noon and stay overnight. Tomorrow morning we'll drive to Hyannis and board the fast ferry to Nantucket."

"Cool. Is Ben going with you?"

"No. This is an all-girls Halloween party. Besides, he's too busy chasing criminals for our police chief."

Someone in the background called Jenna's name.

"Gotta go, Gwen. If you aren't there when I stop home to pack, I'll see you in a few days. Have fun in Nantucket."

"And you enjoy Vermont with your friends."

Jenna hung up.

Gwen put down her phone, leaned down and scooped up Amber, then carried the cat to the kitchen. "I suppose you want your breakfast?"

Amber's ear twitching, the cat endured Gwen's embrace for one second before squirming to be released.

After filling her pet's food and water bowls, Gwen strolled to the bottom of the staircase and looked up.

She'd loved this elegant feature since the day she and Parker rescued it from a New Hampshire salvage warehouse. It was the perfect salute to their converted library.

As she ascended, Gwen reached the midway split and turned right, soon stepping into the sitting room that stretched the length of the rear wall. At the bank of windows, she gazed down into her back garden.

The recent frost could be blamed for the drooping stalks of her beautiful perennials. She decided to tidy the gardens before Tess arrived, but first, Gwen would pack for Nantucket.

She retrieved a wheeled pullman from the loft and carried it to her gabled bedroom at the front corner. Selecting jeans, sweaters, and tops, she tucked them into the luggage, then wrestled it downstairs, placing it near the foyer entrance.

Next... begin the fall clean-up. Exiting through the kitchen sliding door, she crossed the deck and back lawn. In the potting shed, she slid her feet into rubber garden clogs, then grabbed her shears and a collapsible bin.

As she moved from one flower bed to the next, clipping the straggly stems, she once again wondered how Ben would react to her renewed devotion to her departed husband Parker.

She feared Ben would disappear from her life.

Gwen's focus floated around her garden without seeing. Did other widows worry about reconnecting with their husbands in the afterlife? What if they married more than once? Although wedding vows were spoken under the auspices of the church, Gwen held no hope that any priest, minister, or rabbi could resolve her unusual quandary.

If she asked Parker's advice about her relationship with Ben, would the topic be a conflict of interest?

In the past, whenever a problem plagued her, Parker's spirit appeared and offered suggestions. But on this particular day, Gwen decided not to wait for him to show up; instead, she would visit his final resting place.

Though her clean-up project was far from completed, Gwen spread the floral debris in the wooded lot behind the potting shed, stored her tools, and headed out.

***

Gwen parked on the internal road of the memorial cemetery... chosen years before Parker's premature death. Would his spirit come to her here?

As she slid from her driver's seat and approached their patch of ground in the corner, she recalled the day they'd viewed the available plots. When she'd quipped that she didn't like anyone behind her, Parker had laughed, then realized she was serious. They'd purchased the isolated far corner plot and ordered their personalized headstone.

Now, approaching the slanted pink granite, Gwen smiled. Parker's name chiseled on the left heart, Gwen's on the right. Along the bottom ribbon, '*Together Forever.*'

After burying Parker's ashes, Gwen had wept each time she'd visited their final resting place. Now, because his spirit had appeared to her multiple times, she viewed their shared headstone without becoming overly emotional.

Still, she dabbed at her moist eyelashes.

But Parker's ghost hadn't come to her for months. Had their ethereal connection timed out?

Behind her, a man's voice called, "Gwen Andrews?"

She turned to see the cemetery supervisor.

As the man moved toward her, he stretched out his hand. "How are you doing?"

Though Gwen couldn't recall his name, she returned his shake and exchanged small talk. Not wanting to give the impression she was an old lady with hallucinations, Gwen abandoned her plan to call Parker's spirit and excused herself.

***

Back home, stymied by her interrupted plan to contact Parker, Gwen worried that her link to Parker's spirit had possibly been severed.

Redirecting her energies to the bedraggled flower beds, she squatted to clip a stand of drooping grasses. Her peripheral vision spotted movement near the swing adjacent to the back shed and she glanced over.

No mistaking the form hovering there. Parker!

She dropped her clippers and scurried across the lawn, stopping short when she reached his translucent shape.

"Parker, how did you know I needed to talk to you?"

Long ago understanding that a physical hug was impossible, neither attempted an embrace.

In his whispery voice, Parker answered, "I can still sense when you're troubled. What's bothering you?"

As his spirit wavered nearby, Gwen lowered herself to the swing cushions, not yet stored for the season. Clasping her hands in her lap, she began, "Do you remember Ben Snowcrest?"

"Your detective friend?"

"That's him."

"You have a problem with Ben?"

"Not so much a problem as a situation."

"Tell me. I've given you good advice before."

Gwen swallowed. "All right. Do you remember back in June when you pushed my spirit back toward my body, saying it wasn't my time?"

"How could I forget?" Parker quipped.

"Well, in the hospital later, Ben hinted he might propose one day. Now I need to discourage him without losing his friendship."

"I see." Parker floated away, hovering above the flower beds as if inspecting Gwen's initial clean-up efforts. After an excruciating delay, he floated back to her.

"Friends are important, sweetheart... male or female. Explain to Ben that you and I have a special link and that I'll be waiting for you in the afterlife. Assure him you want to remain friends."

Gwen absorbed Parker's words without saying that his advice might be easier said than done.

His ghostly voice went on. "As long as I'm the man you love the most, we'll reconnect one day."

A car door slammed, startling them both.

"That might be my sister," Gwen guessed.

"Or someone else come to visit?" Parker murmured, beginning to evaporate. "I'll leave you to your company."

Gwen turned her attention to the path between her new garage and the corner of her home.

Tess's curly brown head appeared. "Yoo-hoo, I'm here." She hurried past the small pond and came to a stop in front of Gwen, reaching out for a sisterly hug. "Sorry I didn't text. Lost the signal on the turnpike."

Gwen returned her sister's affection, deciding not to mention Parker's visit. Tess hadn't seen him during Madame Eudora's séance, holding tight to her disbelief in the supernatural. Despite her sister's refusal to believe in ghosts, Gwen always hoped that the spirit of Tess's husband Nathan would show himself one day. So far, there'd been no mention of any such occurrence.

"Any traffic problems?"

"Not this time-of-day mid-week." Tess peered at the scattered gardening tools. Would you like some help?"

"My clean-up can wait. We need to shop for costumes. Later, Ben is treating us both to dinner at The Wharf."

"He's sweet. Where's the costume shop?"

"There's one at a plaza near Baylies College. It's close enough to walk, but if we don't find anything there, we can check the Halloween store one town over."

Tess jangled her keys. "I'll drive."

"Let's get you settled first. Jenna's things are in the guest room, so you'll have to share my bed tonight."

"Like when we were kids, Sis. Just don't kick me."

Gwen laughed. "I make no promises."

The two sisters walked to Tess's car, retrieved her luggage, and carried it inside. Mounting the staircase, Tess delivered everything to Gwen's gable bedroom and hurried back down.

Meanwhile, Gwen had texted Ben to let him know that she and Tess looked forward to seeing him at six.

***

Tess's hybrid pulled into the last parking spot at the Harbor Falls party store. Inside, browsers crowded the aisles, carrying various fairy princess, wicked stepmother, and goblin costumes to the front register.

Tess pointed toward the back of the store. "Let's try over there. Oh, and the invitation specified that we are supposed to have masks. Apparently there is going to be a party game to guess who's who."

Gwen laughed. "Well, since we don't know any of the other guests, and they don't know us, that will be tricky." She followed her sister to a discount rack and started to browse through the options.

Tess pulled out a hunchback costume and held it against her tall body. "Yes or no?"

Analyzing the effect, Gwen said, "That'll work if you don't find something better."

After coming upon then rejecting Mutt & Jeff, then Stan & Ollie costumes, Gwen shouted, "Aha!" and held up a white ghost outfit. The package claimed that the mask would induce nightmares. Though she preferred a gentler ghost like her Parker, this one would do.

"What do you think, Tess?"

Her sister backed away. "It's a winner."

"Great. Now let's find a better one for you."

Riffling through the options, Tess shouted, "Eureka!"

Her choice… a black wicked witch outfit, complete with warted mask plus a tall, pointed hat.

"Could we be more cliché?" Tess teased.

Pleased, they paid for their purchases, exited the costume shop, and entered a café three doors down for a bite of lunch.

After a final stop at the hardware store for Gwen to buy a replacement carafe, the sisters headed back to the old library.

Chapter Four

...mid-afternoon, Thursday

Their costumes tucked into their luggage, the sisters retreated to the kitchen.

"Tea?" Gwen asked.

Turning from the glass slider to the back gardens, Tess said, "Let's finish cleaning out your perennial beds first."

"Are you sure?" Gwen asked, not wanting to take advantage of her sister's good nature.

"I wouldn't have offered if I wasn't sure."

"Well, all right. Thanks. With your help, I won't have to deal with it when we return from Nantucket."

Two hours later, the late October sun settled beyond the horizon, forcing the sisters to store the garden tools and lock the shed.

As they stepped onto the upper deck, Gwen checked her watch and waved Tess toward the lounge chairs. "Have a seat and rest for a bit. I'll be right back."

Gwen returned carrying two mugs of warm spiced cider. "Any idea who else Julie invited to her party?"

Pulling out her smart phone, Tess shared the list provided in Julie's email. "No one I know. The invitation does mention a special guest."

"A mystery guest. How enticing,"

"Am I going to see Jenna before we leave?"

"No, we missed her. She was invited to Vermont for the weekend, heading out after her last class. She must have popped back here to pack while we were shopping."

Gwen again checked the time. "We'd better get cleaned up for our dinner with Ben."

***

Six dongs from Gwen's grandmother clock echoed up the staircase, followed by the chime of the doorbell.

Leaving Tess to finish dressing, Gwen hurried downstairs. When she opened the front door, she noted Ben's somber expression. "You don't look all that enthusiastic about taking Tess and me to dinner."

He wagged his head. "Sorry. Tough investigation. A home invasion. The owners were injured, but they'll recover. I can use a distraction."

Gwen's amateur sleuthing forays had taught her that a crime can get under an investigator's skin. She pivoted and shouted up the stairs, "Tess, Ben is here."

"I'm coming." Tess bounded down the staircase and joined them at the front door. "Hi, Ben. I hope you're not upset that I'm stealing Gwen for the weekend."

"Not at all. She's due for a getaway. I certainly haven't been available to take her anywhere."

Gwen peeked past him toward the darkening sky. "Should we walk or drive?"

22

"Walk," Ben advised. "I need the fresh air, and we've got enough time before our reservation."

Snatching an umbrella from the foyer stand, Gwen locked the heavy oak door then followed them down the front walk.

Crossing Library Lane, the trio entered the village green and made their way along the central pathway. Exiting on North Street, they continued down Harbor Hill.

As they passed the Fiction 'n Fables BookStop, Gwen threw her arm in front of Ben and Tess to halt their advance. "Let's go inside. I need to ask Liz for a favor."

***

When Gwen pushed open the shop door, the bell jangled above their heads.

From the register, red-headed Liz spotted them and handed a bag to a customer. "Hi, Gwen, Ben, Tess. What brings you three out on this gloomy night?"

Gwen approached Liz and embraced her best friend, answering, "Dinner at The Wharf."

"Nice." Liz nodded her approval. "Did you drop in to say hello or are you shopping?"

Liz's question tickled Gwen's memory. "Both, I guess. I'm running low on essential oils."

Ben excused himself and wandered toward the books.

Liz headed toward the aromatherapy display. "Which scents do you need?"

"Cinnamon and blood orange."

"Are you still mixing them with frankincense and myrrh?"

"I am. Love the combination of scents."

As Liz reached for Gwen's oils from the array of bottles, Tess picked up a tester and sniffed the contents but said nothing as she returned the bottle to its place.

"How long are you in town, Tess?" Liz asked.

"Just tonight. My college roommate invited me and Gwen to a Halloween party on Nantucket."

Liz's eyebrow lifted. "That'll be an adventure."

"We think so," Gwen added, "which reminds me of the other reason I stopped in. Can you look after Amber while I'm gone?"

"Sure. When are you leaving?"

Tess sniffed and recapped another tester, saying, "Fast ferry first thing in the morning."

"In that case, I'll stop over after I close the shop tomorrow night. I still have your extra house key, Gwen. When will you be back?"

"I imagine either late Sunday or Monday morning," Gwen answered. "I'll text you when we know specifics."

Ben came up beside them, holding a book aloft.

"Found something you like?" Liz asked.

He rotated the volume so they could read the cover. *Leaving Your Job Behind You.*

Gwen chuckled. "Now that's appropriate."

Ben only half-grinned. "I'll dive into it this weekend."

***

Seated at a window table at The Wharf, Gwen noticed Ben

only pushed the baked stuffed scallops around his plate. "Not very hungry?"

His focus shifted to his barely touched food. "Sorry, I haven't had much of an appetite lately."

"Tess and I aren't doing a very good job of distracting you."

Ben sat up straight. "It's not you, it's me." He stabbed a scallop and chewed, a lop-sided grin brightening his face. "This is delicious. Tess, tell me about your college roommate."

Tess recounted her college escapades with Julie decades before, how long it had been since they'd seen each other, and the details of the invitation.

"And me stuck here chasing criminals." Lifting the Fiction 'n Fables bag, Ben removed his book and leafed through the pages. "This sounds good… 'Convincing your old boss to replace you.' I'll read that section first."

"Sounds promising," Gwen remarked, hoping he'd find the advice he needed to free up his retirement hours.

As they sipped after-dinner coffees, Ben sighed with audible satisfaction. "Thanks for diverting me."

When their server brought the bill, Ben handed over his credit card, refusing the sisters' offer to at least pay the tip.

The trio left the restaurant and headed back to Gwen's. As they reached the top of Harbor Hill, lightning lit up the sky, accompanied by the rumble of thunder. Rain poured down.

Gwen opened her umbrella, holding it above their heads as they hurried across the village green. After the oak door was unlocked, all three rushed into the foyer.

Gwen turned to Ben. "Can I offer you something hot to drink? If you'd like coffee, I bought a new carafe this morning."

"Thanks, but I need a good night's sleep more."

Tess headed toward the staircase. "Then I'll say good night, Ben. I need to get out of these wet clothes. Great to see you again. And thanks for dinner."

"Night, Tess. Good to see you." Ben hesitated, then planted a chaste kiss on Gwen's cheek. "Enjoy your Nantucket party. I'm going to miss you this weekend."

Gwen wondered again how she'd preserve their friendship without endangering her link to Parker's spirit. "Hope you find a plus one for the concert. Don't work too hard."

He nodded, then turned and walked out her door.

Gwen watched until his red taillights faded in the curtain of autumn raindrops.

Chapter Five

… early morning, Friday

Early Friday morning, Gwen and Tess drove over the Sagamore Bridge onto Cape Cod. With summer vacationers gone for more than a month, traffic was light.

Entering Hyannis, they made their way to the ferry terminal where an attendant slid their luggage onto a wheeled cart, then handed them a map to the remote parking lot. Within minutes, they'd parked Tess's hybrid and boarded the shuttle bus for the return trip to the terminal.

As the sisters joined the queue of fast ferry passengers, Tess glanced skyward. "I don't like those clouds."

Gwen followed her sister's gaze. "There's a chance of showers on Nantucket, but I don't know about the crossing."

Extending her ticket to a crew member for scanning, Tess asked, "Are you expecting a smooth ride?"

He grinned and held one finger high in the air. "A bit of a stiff wind this morning. There's always a chance of a pop-up shower, but I'm not expecting one today."

Nodding, the two sisters moved into the lower level and sat at a water-view booth. When the ferry finally pulled away from the dock, they watched the mainland slowly disappear, replaced by relatively smooth water.

Gwen asked, "How will we get from the ferry landing to Julie's cottage?"

"Thanks for the reminder. I'll text we're on our way, and she'll be waiting for us at the dock."

For the next hour, neither sister succumbed to the gentle rocking until the ferry was securely moored, and they disembarked down the ramp.

A woman's voice shouted, "Tess! Gwen! Over here."

Still spry for a baby boomer, Tess sprinted toward her college roommate. "Julie, you look great."

Playfully swishing her blonde ponytail, Julie said, "Thanks. I'm loving island life."

Gwen stepped closer. "Thanks for including me."

Julie gave Gwen a one-armed squeeze. "You were always so tolerant when Tess brought me home. Let's go."

Spotting the luggage carts, Gwen and Tess located theirs by its number, and dropped their pieces to the dock boards. Their wheels clattering across the uneven surfaces, they followed Julie across cobbled streets to a parking lot.

When Julie pointed her key fob at a lime green Jeep, the doors clicked open.

"Well," Tess commented, "you're not going to sneak around the island driving that."

Julie laughed. "I don't drive much. When the carpenter needed my opinion about materials, I rode in his truck."

Luggage stowed in the back, Julie steered them through several intersections and headed east.

Impressed by the individuality of the island homes they passed, Gwen winced when she spotted massive cookie cutter buildings sprawling in a field. "What are those?"

Julie glanced over. "Subsidized housing. Millionaires have been buying up real estate, pricing locals out of the market."

They rode in silence until Tess pointed to the overcast sky. "Is a storm going to interrupt your party tonight?"

Flapping her hand in dismissal, Julie said, "The weather gurus mentioned a system developing to our south, but they always forecast doom and gloom. Most of the time, storms fizzle before they reach Nantucket, so islanders tend to ignore the predictions. The last major storm to make landfall was Arthur in 2014. And in 2018, four inches of rain flooded downtown. But nothing that scary since I bought my cottage."

Julie maneuvered a miniature traffic circle that marked the center of Sconset, exiting on the road heading north. She soon turned onto a patterned driveway that curved toward a three-story Victorian with a wide front veranda and a side sunporch.

Her mouth open, Tess gazed out the windshield. "You call this a cottage?"

Laughing, Julie said, "I've learned that the term cottage simply means a summer place and doesn't refer to the size. Many folks on Nantucket are seasonal residents." She slid the gearshift into the park position and turned off the ignition.

Tess scrambled from the passenger seat and stood with her hands on her hips. "Your cottage is magnificent, but why such a big house if you're the only one living here?"

"I couldn't resist its charm. This property sat empty for years and needed lots of TLC. But I saw its potential and negotiated a lower price." She pointed to the top of the house. "The third-floor attic is now my art studio. I've resurrected my love of painting."

"Can't wait to see it," Tess murmured.

The sisters followed their hostess through the oversized front door, painted a charming sea green to contrast against the grey weather-worn shingles.

In the foyer, Julie waved toward the kitchen on her right, then the dining room on their left. French doors opened onto a sunporch beyond.

Leading them down a hallway beside the central staircase, Julie brought them into a living room with a continuous run of windows and sliding glass door facing the Atlantic Ocean.

"This view never gets old," Julie said, her tone wistful.

Gwen studied the restless waves beyond a stone patio and the shallow lawn, pointing toward a platform with wooden steps that disappeared. "Where do those lead?"

"From the top of the bluff down to the beach," Julie explained, then swept both arms wide. "These windows face southeast. One of my walking friends joked that if I drew a straight line across the Atlantic, I'd find myself in North Africa's Sahara Desert."

Chuckling, Julie turned toward the sisters. "One last piece of house history. Rumor has it that the spirit of a sea captain roams these rooms, though I've never encountered him."

Before Gwen could decide whether to mention Parker's ghost, Julie continued. "The captain is the reason for my special guest. Follow me, and I'll introduce you."

Chapter Six

… late morning, Friday

Backtracking, they entered the kitchen, where an elegant woman was pressing cookie cutters into dough.

Julie called, "Ursula? I'd like you to meet my college roommate Tess and her sister Gwen."

When Ursula turned, her perfectly made-up face spread into a grin. "Gwen Andrews? Can that be you?"

Though this special guest looked familiar, Gwen couldn't quite place her.

"Oh, I know why you don't recognize me." Ursula grabbed a hand towel, piled her flowing black hair atop her head, and held the makeshift turban in place.

The woman's name took shape. "Madame Eudora?"

"Yes. Yes. That's my professional name. So good to see you again, Gwen."

Julie's eyes widened. "You two know each other?"

"Gwen once did me a favor by allowing my séance to be relocated to her home."

Ursula glanced back at Gwen. "My cousin is hoping I can summon the ghost of her sea captain."

Ursula picked up a dark nut and grated it atop the cookie shapes, then slid the sheet into the oven and set the timer.

"When should we hold our séance, Julie?"

Tapping one finger against her chin, Julie replied, "At tonight's party if my other guests are curious. We'll see." She pointed toward the waiting luggage. "I'm going to settle these sisters in the guest suite. Be right back."

Ursula lifted her chin and mimicked the lofty voice of a golden age movie star. "I await your return."

Waving off Ursula's antics, Julie led Gwen and Tess up the staircase, pausing at the second-floor landing. "Leave your luggage here for a second. I want to show you my new studio."

They followed her up one more flight and through a frosted door into an oversized space with slanted ceiling. Light dimmed by the cloudy sky streamed through the windows of both dormers, each outfitted with window seats.

"Self-contained solar panels on the roof power either heat or cooling, so we didn't need to add baseboard or ductwork to the original attic. Julie indicated rooftop skylights above their heads. "I can open those panels if I want fresh air,"

Tess turned around once, then a second time. "What a marvelous studio."

"Isn't it though?" Julie's joy was obvious.

"This required skilled craftsmen," Gwen added.

"Fortunately, my contractor hired a wonderful carpenter who lives a few houses down the bluff walk."

"Handy," Gwen commented. "Years ago, my husband, who was an architect, converted an abandoned library into our home."

"That's where Ursula held her séance?"

33

"Yes, that's the place."

"I'd love to meet him and tour your unusual home."

A spark coursed through Gwen's body. "You're welcome anytime so I can show off his talent, but my Parker died a few years ago."

Julie laid her hand on Gwen's arm. "I'm so sorry."

Again, Gwen debated whether to divulge the existence of Parker's ghost. She decided not to mention him. No need to compete with Julie's sea captain.

The moment vanished when Julie pointed to an empty easel angled toward the window. "I'm going to attempt a seaside painting. My technique with brushes and paint is a bit rusty, but I'm excited to try." Julie lifted her eyes to both sisters. "Okay. Let's get you two settled."

They descended one flight to the second floor and Julie led them into an oversized space that boasted two queen beds, a sitting room, and its own bath.

"This suite was created by removing the wall between two of the four original bedrooms," Julie explained. "Other than Ursula, you two are my first guests. After this weekend, I'll invite others to visit."

Gwen strolled to an ocean-facing window, again mesmerized by the movement of the waves. The sun strained to break though the overcast sky. Dark clouds hovered in the distance. Remembering Julie's lack of concern for a weather system developing to their south, Gwen dismissed Tess's worry about a storm interfering with the party.

"I need to get back to Ursula," Julie announced. "After you've unpacked, join us in the kitchen. We'll put you to work preparing the party food."

***

Gwen and Tess hung up their costumes and each filled a dresser drawer before storing their luggage in the large walk-in closet.

Glancing over, Tess commented, "You and Ben seemed a bit awkward at dinner last night."

After she sat on the queen bed where she'd tossed her PJ's, Gwen debated how to share her relationship challenge with Tess. But if not her sister, who else? Simplifying the problem, Gwen said, "Ben and I haven't seen each other much over the last several months."

"Why is that?"

"I mentioned that Ben retired back in June?"

Tess nodded, waving Gwen to continue.

"Well, the Harbor Falls police chief continues to call Ben to assist on new cases. They've been friends for years, and Ben doesn't want to endanger their friendship, so he hasn't refused the requests. You must have picked up on his frustration."

"Hard to miss, but what are you *not* telling me?"

Gwen sensed no harm in revealing the simplest explanation. "Ben has hinted he wants more than friendship, and I'm just not ready."

Unwilling to burden her sister further with a debate only Gwen herself could untangle, she didn't mention the afterlife and instead put Tess on the spot. "What about you? Any interesting men since Nathan passed?"

A half-grin brightened Tess's expression. "The only men in my life are my doctor, my dentist, and the mailman."

Gwen considered her sister's evasive answer and raised an eyebrow. "And are you seeing one of them for more personal reasons?"

Tess fell on the other bed laughing.

If Gwen's sister was lonely for male companionship, she hid it well.

Chapter Seven

… early afternoon, Friday

When the sisters descended the staircase and entered the kitchen, Gwen sniffed the air. "What are you two cooking in here? It smells delicious."

Ursula closed the fridge door. "Might be the nutmeg on my Halloween cookies."

"Or," Julie suggested as she retrieved bowls from a glass-fronted cabinet, "you could be smelling our lunch of clam chowder, side salad, and freshly baked bread."

Next to Gwen, the stove timer dinged. She grabbed a pair of oven mitts. "I'll get that," then removed garlic sticks and transferred them to a waiting breadbasket.

Tess covered them with a handy towel. "Where to?"

"The dining room," Julie answered, pointing her chin.

Following Tess, Ursula carried individual salads.

When Julie joined them, Gwen commented on the whaling motif. "Your tableware is so Nantucket."

Julie chuckled, "I came across these dishes at a tag sale. Couldn't resist them."

When the chowder had cooled, Gwen sampled her first taste. "Delicious, Julie. If you don't mind me asking, how do you and Ursula know each other?"

Poising her spoon in midair, Julie answered, "She's a distant cousin on my grandmother's side. We reconnected at a family gathering and I suggested she visit after I completed my renovations."

Gwen grinned. "I find it amusing that your timing coincides with Halloween."

Ursula laughed. "We thought it appropriate."

"Forgive my curiosity," Gwen inquired, "but your name is quite unusual."

"Easy to explain," the medium responded. "My mother was a big fan of Ursula Andress."

Tess joined the conversation. "Wasn't she the actress who emerged from the ocean in a white bikini? I don't remember the name of the movie."

"That was *Dr. No*," Ursula supplied, "the first James Bond movie. A few years later, the actress's bikini sold at auction for half a million."

"Amazing what people will pay," Tess commented before continuing to eat her lunch.

"Younger movie goers associate my name with the sea witch in *The Little Mermaid* movie."

"Audiences change with time," Gwen commented. "When we met before, I knew you as Madame Eudora."

"Yes, I go by both. When my mother realized I wasn't imagining the visitors to my childhood bedroom, she understood that I'd inherited my grandmother's sensitivity to spirits and jokingly dubbed me Madame Eudora. It stuck."

Julie added, "Ursula's grandmother was my great aunt from the other branch of the family. That likely explains why I haven't seen my sea captain's ghost."

Ursula turned back to the sisters. "From an early age, I held séances for family members, close friends, and neighbors well into my teenage years. Eventually, I published a book as Madame Eudora about my experiences under the title *They're Not Really Gone*."

Julie turned her gaze toward Gwen. "Now tell me the story about my cousin holding her séance at your home."

Happy to oblige, Gwen explained the circumstances. "I spotted Ursula's book at a local bookshop to publicize her upcoming séance in Harbor Falls. I signed up with no idea that I'd end up hosting the event."

"How did that happen?" Julie asked.

"Rancid smoke from a new cigar bar found its way into my friend Liz's bookshop next door. With her space tainted, she asked me to substitute as hostess."

Ursula sat forward. "Gwen's home was a perfect venue."

"Thanks," Gwen said. "I thought so, too."

Tess glanced at the other three. "I happened to be visiting Gwen for a few days, so sat in at that séance, but I didn't see any ghosts."

"Not everyone can, Tess," Ursula soothed as she switched her attention back to Gwen. "But your sister did."

Gwen understood that Ursula was referring to Parker's antics during the séance. He'd waved to make the candles flicker and blown on the hair of the other women, each action making them squeal with delight.

"I found your book fascinating," Gwen went on. "Are you planning a second one?"

Ursula shook her head. "Not at the moment, though I keep detailed notes of each event. I'm hoping the party guests tonight agree to the evening séance. Their reactions will add another story to my collection."

When the conversation dwindled, Gwen waved her hand toward the kitchen. "Speaking of the party, Julie, you said you'd put us to work."

"I did say that. Now that we've finished our lunch, we can prepare the rest of the party food." Julie stacked the soup bowls and led the way to the kitchen, pointing to a far corner. "That rented witch's cauldron needs washing before we fill it with a cocktail called Bloody Vampire Bite.

"Now that's an interesting name," Gwen said, truly amused. "I'll take care of cleaning that."

Tess looked around. "How can I help?"

"I didn't quite finish decorating out front. There are still three boxes stacked in the entrance hall."

"I'm on it." Tess disappeared through the doorway.

While Tess was busy outside, Gwen washed and dried the cauldron, found a perfect location on the living room sideboard, then arranged the warming trays for appetizers.

Next she assisted Ursula with the preparation of chicken strips shaped like fingers, ribs and mini hot dogs in red sauces,

Jalapeno popper mummies, zombie brain cupcakes, and bloody brownies. An astounding array of appetizers and desserts.

Julie stood at the kitchen island blending a creamy beverage that looked familiar.

Gwen peeked over her shoulder. "What's this?"

"Eggnog with rum and fresh nutmeg."

"What about guests who prefer non-alcoholic drinks?"

"Glad you reminded me. Could you fill that tub with bags of ice? Then add the bottles of water and soda that are on the basement steps?"

Gwen nodded and set about her next task.

By the time they'd finalized the preparations, the late-day October sun had set beyond the clouds.

Julie signaled Gwen and Ursula. "Let's check Tess's handiwork." At the front door, she touched a switch, turning on the veranda's orange bulb and they walked outside.

Googly eyes on black balloons were alternated with black bats on orange balloons. Fake cobwebs floated between festooning the archway. Battery-powered candles glowed inside plastic pumpkins. Paper ghosts fluttered on sticks.

"Very festive," Julie commented. "Good job."

Tess chuckled. "Brought to you by your own decorations."

"It's getting close to party time," Julie pointed out. "We'd better go inside and change."

They all rushed to the second floor, soon meeting at the bottom of the staircase to marvel at each other's costumes.

Tess twirled in her witch outfit with wart-covered mask.

Ursula's sultry voice emerged from a blood-streaked face and a short brown wig under a nurse's cap that concealed her black tresses as she said, "Definitely spooky, Tess."

Julie wore a nun costume, her blonde hair covered by the black veil, her face hidden beneath a mask with glowing eyes. She twirled her rosary beads in a menacing circle. "You may need some more blood on your nurse's uniform, Ursula. Maybe we can stain it with some of the punch after we make it."

Ursula laughed. "I'm an expert at staining anything I wear. Is the recipe cranberry juice and vodka?"

Julie nodded, and Ursula began pouring the two liquid ingredients into the cauldron.

Gwen, in her ghost attire, added lemon juice and muddled blackberries.

Julie placed hors d'oeuvres on the warming trays.

Tess clustered cold canapes atop platters of ice.

When the food and drinks were set, Julie turned on eerie music, adding a Halloween mood.

The others draped colorful scarves across lampshades to create a spooky atmosphere.

All they needed now were guests.

Chapter Eight

… the Halloween Party, Friday night

Promptly at six, revelers began to arrive, some from the front veranda, others through the sliding glass door at the stone patio that faced the Atlantic Ocean.

All wearing different costumes, the guests drifted toward the party food, then wandered the living room to inspect Julie's décor as they munched.

After a polite interval, Julie stepped onto the raised platform fronting the slider and clapped her hands. "Time to guess who's who, ladies. Me first."

Little Orphan Annie, a young woman even shorter than Gwen, moved forward. "That's easy, Julie. You answered the front door, and you added another platter of food. Love your creative appetizers."

Whoops of *'take it off'* soon followed.

Obligingly, Julie removed her mask and the nun's black veil, shaking out her blonde tresses. "Lucky guess, Orphan Annie, but one of my house guests could have opened the door and also carried in more food."

"But you also initiated this party game," someone else called out.

"You've got me there," Julie conceded.

Behind her, a flash of lightning bleached the sky.

Everyone gasped when the boom of thunder rattled the multiple windowpanes.

As the night sky theater continued, Julie flapped one hand. "Pay no attention. I'm sure the storm will disintegrate before it reaches us. Let's continue our guessing game."

She motioned to the lucky guesser. "Get up here, Little Orphan Annie."

Someone yelled, "Gotta be you, Evie Henderson."

Laughing, the petite woman tore off her wig and mask, revealing her own mop of auburn hair. "I'm too easy. No short jokes or I'll mis-bag your groceries next time you come through my register at the mid-island grocery store."

Chuckling, Julie handed Evie a pre-labeled name tag.

Evie tore off the backing and slapped the label onto the bodice of her costume. "Great idea. Who's next?"

Mary Poppins came forward, complete with umbrella, white gloves, and a perky hat atop her own grey hair. After several wild guesses, when no one solved her identity, the woman's British accent identified herself as Hester Lawrence, a volunteer at the Historical Association. She'd met Julie while researching the captain's home.

Tinker Bell flapped her arms, her wings tapping the others as she moved through the group. After a few wrong guesses, she laughed. "Didn't think you'd know me." She removed her mask. "My name is Jasmine Nash, and I work at the farmstand on the southern coast."

Another guest twirled the tail of her leopard jumpsuit and Julie said, "I'd know those shapely legs anywhere. Nikki Quinn from the yoga studio?"

Correctly guessed, the woman unmasked and stuck her nametag on her costume.

Next came a disco dancer wearing tall white boots, tossing her long brown wig this way and that.

Evie chimed in. "Is that you, Crystal Young?"

Striking a pose from *Saturday Night Fever*, the woman nodded then removed her disguise. "You got me. And I just have to say, as a stay-at-home mom raising pre-school twins and a five-month-old baby, thank you, Julie, for inviting me to this grown-up party. My husband is babysitting our brood to give me a break."

The veiled 1920s flapper with headband, strappy shoes, and pink cheeks quietly took the spotlight next. When no one could guess who she was, she pushed the veil aside and softly spoke her name as Rose Griffin, adding she worked at a downtown gift shop before hiding behind the group.

The other guests included "Bad Sandy" from *Grease* wearing a black bodysuit that enhanced her trim figure. Her first name was also Sandy, her last name Owens. She'd met Julie at the post office, and they'd become friends.

Lastly, a plump woman in a striped prisoner outfit dragged ball and chain until she halted near the sofa, smoothing the throw tossed along the back. "I'm Molly Burns. Not to brag, but Julie bought this beautiful piece at my textile shop." As the women swarmed closer to touch the woven fabric, Molly handed a business card to each one. Several promised they'd drop by the shop soon.

"Nice marketing ploy, Molly," Julie called out. "Now, it's time for you to meet my house guests."

Tess swished her black witch costume as she edged her way forward, quickly removing her warty mask. "My name is Tess. Julie and I were college roommates back in the day. And this is my younger sister Gwen."

Beneath her white flowing ghost costume, Gwen waved her arms in true party spirit – pun intended – emitting spooky noises until she stood beside Tess.

"And, finally, my guest of honor. My cousin Ursula."

In her RN uniform, Ursula nodded and bowed.

Julie clapped her hands to quiet the group. "I'd suggest a contest for favorite costume, but I love them all."

She then linked arms with Ursula. "Before you ghouls and goblins devour the remaining party food, I'd like my cousin to introduce her alternate persona."

Fully aware that Ursula was about to reveal her skill as a medium, Gwen waited to see how the others would react to the offer of a séance.

The approaching storm raging beyond the darkness outside provided the perfect backdrop.

Chapter Nine

… mid evening, Friday

"First of all," Ursula announced, "a brief history of my childhood." She repeated the details shared with Gwen and Tess during lunch.

"And that," Ursula concluded, "brings us to a question about the remainder of our evening. Are any of you aware that some claim Julie's house is haunted?"

Sandy raised her hand. "Given Nantucket's whaling heritage, there's no shortage of ghost stories."

Red-headed Evie stepped closer. "If you're suggesting a séance, count me in."

When no one else spoke, Julie said, "I'll bring out the desserts while the rest of you decide."

Aware that not everyone believed in spirits – Tess among them – Gwen waited to see how many party guests were willing to sit around Madame Eudora's table.

A quiet buzz filled the room.

After a polite interval, Julie again moved onto the platform and claimed their attention. "I'm anxious to discover if my ghost is the sea captain who built this house, but you may not share my curiosity."

Ursula swept her gaze through the group. "Feel free to decline but raise your hand if you're feeling brave."

Most of the guests inched their hands into the air.

Crystal stepped forward. "Sounds like fun, but I need to get back home and rescue my husband from our kids."

"That's perfectly fine," Julie soothed.

"But I don't want to hold up your séance," Crystal continued, "so I'll say my goodbyes now. Thanks for a great party, Julie, and good luck connecting with your captain. You can tell me what happened next time we bump into each other on the beach." Crystal gripped the handle of the sliding door and yanked it sideways, allowing a gust of cool air to swirl inside and ruffle everyone's hair.

Julie reached for a switch. Outside, a light blinked on, barely cutting into the darkness. "Be careful. Looks like the weather forecasters were finally right about a storm."

A bolt of lightning brightened the young mother's face. "My house isn't far. Text me next time you're walking." Moving beyond the glow of the orange bulb, Crystal merged with the darkness.

Closing the door against the blustery wind, Julie faced the remaining guests. "Before we begin, I'll share the encounters others have experienced in this house."

Someone pounded on the glass sliding door.

Startled, Julie jumped and said, "Crystal must have forgotten something."

Once again sliding open the door, Julie stepped through the opening and lowered her voice, though Gwen was near enough to hear her brusque greeting.

"What are you doing here, Sylvia?"

An older woman – dressed haphazardly, her hair wispy and unkempt, her lined face shadowed by the garish orange lightbulb, stared at Julie, snapping, "Where's my husband?"

Visibly stiffening, Julie said, "I don't know why you think Wyatt is here. If you'll excuse me, I have guests." She grasped the handle to slide the door closed.

The woman's slippered foot thrust into the opening, her bloodshot eyes glaring at the costumed women staring back at her. "Halloween party, Julie? My invitation must have gotten lost in the mail."

Julie's face reddening, she stammered, "I... I didn't think you'd be interested, Sylvia. Would you like a cup of eggnog?"

Sylvia answered by jerking the slider open wide enough to stumble inside, nearly tripping off the elevated platform.

The astonished partygoers parted like the Red Sea, creating a pathway to the sideboard.

Julie followed and ladled eggnog into a skull-shaped mug, then grated nutmeg on top and extended the beverage to Sylvia.

Taking a swallow, the brash woman coughed and sputtered. "Way too much nutmeg, Julie. You trying to get me high?"

"What do you mean, get you high?" Julie challenged, disbelief in her tone. Without waiting for an explanation, she held out a nearly empty platter. "Pumpkin cookie?"

Sylvia waved it off. "I'll pass on that silly dessert, but I need a chat with you, Julie. In private unless you want your guests to hear what a slut you are."

Molly barreled forward. "You're very demanding for a party crasher." Turning to Julie, Molly said, "Before you go off alone with this woman, are you aware she's drunk?"

"I am *not* drunk," Sylvia hissed, attempting to stomp her foot, only to wobble, nearly losing her balance.

Molly waved her hand in front of her own nose. "You might think your mouthwash camouflaged the fumes, but I could smell your liquor from across the room. You'd better start taking care of yourself, Sylvia, or you'll never know where that handsome husband of yours has run off to."

Sylvia backed up, her face puckering. "You've got your nerve to say those things to me."

As Gwen watched the confrontation, Molly stood her ground and barked, "Julie told you that your husband isn't here, so it's time for you to leave."

Julie placed her hand on Molly's arm. "I appreciate your intervention, but I'll take it from here." She signaled Ursula. "Would you take our guests up to the third-floor studio and wait for me?"

Though Ursula tossed a questioning look at Julie, she nodded and ushered the others toward the staircase.

Hester hesitated. "Julie, would you like me to share the history of your cottage with the others?"

"Great idea, Hester, thanks. I shouldn't be long. I'll see you upstairs in a bit."

Uneasy about the inebriated Sylvia, Gwen whispered to Tess. "Should we leave them down here by themselves?"

"Julie's a scrapper from way back. I'm not concerned."

Accepting that Tess knew her old roommate better than anyone in the room ever would, Gwen shrugged.

Heading toward the bottom of the staircase, they blended with the others and listened as Molly asked Hester, "When was this house built?"

"In the early 1800s," Hester began as she mounted the first tread. Her polished British accent somehow elevated the details. "The original owner was a successful sea captain with several whaling vessels…"

Chapter Ten

… mid evening, Friday

Fascinated by Hester's history lesson, Gwen didn't notice the passage of time until Julie swept into her studio, dabbing a paper towel on her blonde tresses.

Ursula rushed over. "Are you okay? I was about to come looking for you."

Dropping onto the artist's chair near her empty easel, Julie said, "I'm fine, but it's begun to rain."

Tess moved closer. "What did that Sylvia want?"

Julie's shoulders lifted and dropped. "This wasn't the first time she's accused me of having an affair with her husband."

As the other guests formed a circle around their hostess, Gwen asked, "What's your connection to Wyatt?"

Pushing to her feet, Julie moved to the nearest window and gazed out into the stormy night. "He was the carpenter who created this studio from a dusty attic, but he completed the project a month or so ago."

Evie chimed in, "When Wyatt updated my kitchen last year, the same thing happened. One day, Sylvia showed up drunk and accused me of sleeping with him."

Julie nodded and tossed her damp paper towel into a nearby wastebasket. "Wyatt has mentioned his wife's drinking problem. She just now threatened to call the Civic Association and complain about our party noise."

Nikki detached her leopard's tail and placed it on a nearby chair. "We haven't been at all rowdy. Is Sylvia still outside?"

Julie shrugged one shoulder.

"Well, I'm going down and ask her not to make a fuss. I'll offer to walk her home and she'll forget about reporting us. Anyone coming with me?"

When no one volunteered, Nikki hurried out, her footsteps echoing as she raced down two floors.

Ursula waved after her. "Let's wait for Nikki to rejoin us, and then I'll begin our séance."

Julie paused for only a second. "That's the polite thing to do. Hester, did you finish the house history?"

"For the most part," Hester replied.

"Thank you for filling the time. Let me show everyone an incredibly special discovery." Julie waved them to the opposite end of her studio, pausing before a framed painting. "Wyatt and I came upon this portrait while we were cleaning out this attic space so he could create this studio."

The way Julie spoke Wyatt's name, Gwen suspected he'd become more than her friend. Was Sylvia right to suspect an affair or was she simply an insecure wife? Julie wasn't the first woman Sylvia had accused of having an affair with the man.

The classic love triangle – even if it existed only in Sylvia's alcohol-saturated brain – reminded Gwen of her own delicate balance between Parker's spirit and the living Ben.

The comparison echoed uncomfortably. *Were other widows unfaithful if their partner no longer held a physical form?*

Ben remained in Gwen's mind. She'd been so distracted since she'd boarded the ferry with Tess that morning, she hadn't given him even one second of thought. Was he reading his new book? Would it be too late to call him after the séance ended and the partygoers went home?"

Excited voices drew Gwen from her personal challenge to concentrate on the somber man in the portrait. "He's very stern, Julie. Do you know who he is?"

Julie beamed. "Meet Captain Percy Tiffin. His name is written on the back of the canvas."

Clasping her hands behind her back, Hester leaned forward and peered at the lower front corner. "That's interesting. The artist didn't sign his work. But the style is similar to other 19th century portraits hanging in our Whaling Museum gallery."

Behind them, Nikki swept into the studio, her wet hair dripping on her leopard leotard. "The storm has arrived in full force with all its fury."

On cue, heavy drops pelted against the studio windows. Lightning flashed and thunder boomed much closer than it had just a few minutes before.

When Julie glanced up at the skylights, another flash softened the lines in her baby-boomer face. "Perfect timing to share my ghost stories. But first, Nikki, let's dry your hair," Julie opened a door to reveal a compact bathroom, reached in and handed a dry towel to Nikki.

Dramatically lowering her voice, Julie began. "Mind you, everything I'm about to tell you was experienced by others. Many of the events took place right here when this space was the original attic. Visitors and residents alike heard furniture scraping across the hardwood or the thud of boxes dropping onto the floorboards or windowpanes clattering." She inhaled a noisy breath. "Doors slamming, unscrewed lightbulbs, windows left ajar after they'd been firmly locked. But none of the stories ever included anyone actually seeing the ghost. I'm only guessing that he's my sea captain Percy."

"Is there more than one ghost?" Nikki asked as she folded the damp towel.

Before Julie could answer, Ursula stepped forward. "That's what we hope to discover this evening." She reached over and touched Julie's arm. "I believe you planned our séance around your dining room table, cousin, but we might make better connections in this studio since this is where most of the activity occurred."

Julie's eyes widened. "That makes sense, Ursula." She glanced around at the others. "We can't haul my dining room table up two flights, but if you'll all follow me to the basement, we can carry up card tables and folding chairs stored down there."

Chapter Eleven

… late evening, Friday

After following Julie into the dank cellar, the women wrestled the portable card tables and folding chairs up to the first floor. As they paused to catch their breath, a loud tapping echoed from the direction of the patio door.

"What now?" Julie grumbled. "You can either wait for me to see who this is or continue up to the studio."

Molly unfolded the chair she carried and sat down. "I vote to rest and find out who's knocking so late."

"Me, too," Hester agreed.

The group quieted as Julie once again slid open the glass door, revealing that the raindrops had slowed to a lazy bounce off the patio flagstones, though in the distance lightning split the night sky and thunder rumbled ominously.

A thoroughly soaked man stood on the patio.

"Wyatt?" Julie said, her tone one of surprise. "What are you doing out on this stormy night?"

Gwen's ears perked up. So this ruggedly handsome man was the infamous Wyatt?

Despite his waterlogged clothing and the rain dipping from his salt and pepper hair onto his broad shoulders, every female in the room focused on the latest visitor.

His eyebrows lifted. "Julie? I didn't recognize you in that nun's outfit." He leaned sideways to look at the costumed women staring at him. "Are you having a Halloween party?"

"Yes. But tell me why you're here?"

"Sorry to interrupt, but have you seen Sylvia?"

"She was here earlier looking for you."

His expression darkened. "She thought I was here?"

"Apparently."

"How long ago was that?"

Julie glanced at her watch. "I'd guess at least an hour."

Wyatt gazed at her with an unreadable expression. "When I returned from my Al-Anon meeting, Sylvia wasn't in the house. Her car is still parked in the garage. Now you've told me she wandered up here. She's been drinking again, Julie. I'm worried about her." Wyatt stuck his hand out past the patio overhang. "The rain's nearly stopped. Is there any chance you can help me search for her?"

Julie waved down her body to indicate her costume, her voice quiet but firm. "Sorry, but I'm not dressed to wander around in the dark wetness. Did you call the police?"

Nodding, Wyatt slid his rough-looking hand through his salt & pepper hair. "The dispatcher said they're short-handed, plus Sylvia hasn't been missing for twenty-four hours."

Tess swished forward in her witch's costume. "It's a nasty night, Julie. I hate to think of anyone out in this weather, and she was very unstable. I can change and help him search."

Gwen piped up. "I can, too."

57

When Wyatt's eyebrows half-lifted to form a sad puppy-dog look, Julie caved. "Oh, all right. Give the three of us a few minutes to change. I'll grab some flashlights."

Julie turned to face her remaining guests. "I doubt if you brought a change of clothes, and I don't expect the rest of you to ruin your outfits."

Ursula said, "We'll stay here and get everything set up in your studio."

"Thank you. We shouldn't be long."

***

Five minutes later, Gwen, Tess, and Julie bounded down the staircase in jeans and sweatshirts.

On the patio, Julie lifted the lid of a storage box and removed three flashlights, switching them on to check the strength of the batteries.

Handing one each to Tess and Gwen, they followed Wyatt across the shallow lawn to the bluff walk.

He turned to face them. "I searched left and right as I headed this way, so we should continue north."

When Tess made a move toward the platform, Julie put out a hand to stop her. "That wood is slippery when wet, so let's confine our search to both sides of the path."

Swinging their beams in a wide arch, they progressed slowly along the dirt surface, stepping gingerly around the puddles collected from the runoff.

Walking behind Wyatt, Julie said to his back. "You're assuming Sylvia came this way."

He shrugged. "Like I said, I have no idea where she could have gone after she left your place. You confirmed she was drunk. I need to find her and get her back home."

"Maybe she's already there," Gwen suggested.

"I can only hope," he commented.

After another five minutes, Julie held up her hand.

"I'm sorry, Wyatt, but I have to get back to my guests."

"I can't blame you, Julie. Sorry for pulling you away from your party. Thanks to all three of you for helping me. I'll continue my search from here."

"Hasn't the Bluff Walk eroded up ahead?" Julie asked.

"You're right. I'll have to switch over to Baxter Road toward the lighthouse."

"Maybe you'll bump into Sylvia out there."

"I can only hope," he said as he hurried off at a quick pace, shining his flashlight right then left until he disappeared around the bend.

***

Returning to Julie's cottage, they removed their wet sneakers and hurried up to the studio.

"Did you find Sylvia?" Ursula's called.

Gwen did a double take as she rounded the corner.

Ursula had transformed into Madame Eudora, her long hair tucked beneath a black turban. The metal beads on her flowing purple gown reflected the ambient light. Oversized metal baubles dangled at her ears. Heavy black eye liner added a dramatic effect.

"We didn't see any sign of her," Julie answered. "Wyatt's continuing his search. Hopefully, he'll find her back home."

As Ursula's theatrical eyes roamed the gathered women, she asked, "Is it too late to hold our séance?"

A resounding chorus of 'No' echoed off the slanted ceiling and skylights.

"In that case," Ursula continued, "please choose a seat. Julie, if you could please lower the lights."

Ursula… as Madame Eudora… struck a match and leaned over to light white candles in silver candlesticks. Reaching into her satchel, she removed small plates, filling both with sand.

Withdrawing two dried sprigs, she touched another match to the first and quickly blew out the flame. The plume of fragrant smoke wafted upward as her hypnotic voice murmured, "Sage to deter the negative spirits among us."

She repeated the ceremony with the second braid. "Sweet grass to welcome positive spirits and angels."

The stage set, Madame Eudora eased into the head chair. "Let's all join hands." She recited the following chant three times in succession:

"May the light and energy of these candles remove all fear, negativity, and doubt.

May these candles attract positive energy to the women gathered here this evening.

For the highest good of all and for the good of the universe, so be it, so be it, so be it."

Gwen recognized the white candles, the smoldering herbs, and the chant as repetitions of Ursula's ceremony during the séance in Gwen's dining room years before.

Next, Madame Eudora invited any spirits in the vicinity to reveal themselves.

When the blustery wind rattled the windowpanes, everyone gasped but no transparent beings materialized.

After repeatedly cajoling the captain to show himself, Ursula glanced at Julie. "I'm sorry, cousin. Either your captain isn't here or he's stubborn about appearing."

Releasing the hands of the other women, Julie stood up. "Or maybe he doesn't like my changes to his home."

"I rarely hold a séance with no results," Ursula said apologetically. "We can try again this weekend if you want."

"Maybe," Julie replied, disappointment evident.

Evie indicated the card tables and chairs. "Want some help carrying these down to your basement?"

"Thanks," Julie answered, "but it was enough that you all helped carry them up here in the first place. There's no rush. I'll take care of them tomorrow."

Julie ushered her guests down the stairs. "Just because our séance didn't connect with my captain doesn't mean the party is over. Please indulge in the remaining goodies."

Not long after that, Molly licked her fingers and moved toward the patio door, making a show of hefting her ball and chain. "Thanks for a great party, Julie. I'm expecting an early delivery tomorrow, so I'll say goodnight."

Because Gwen happened to be standing on the raised platform, she stopped Molly. "I hope to visit your shop before returning to the mainland."

"I'd love to show you some items on display that you might like." With that, Molly disappeared beyond the orange glow.

Nikki, her leopard leotard now dry, headed out the patio door, saying, "Loved the séance, Julie. Sorry you didn't connect with your captain. Be sure to bring your guests by the yoga studio. Good night."

Every few minutes, another guest peeled herself away from the group that remained and headed home.

Petite Evie waved goodbye, then Hester, promising to check the portraits at the Whaling Museum she thought were a similar style to Captain Percy Tiffin's portrait.

Sandy offered a ride to Tinker Bell Jasmine, who pretended to fly as she followed Sandy out the front door.

Rose, the last to leave, exited quietly, whispering goodbye so faintly she could barely be heard.

Stepping out to the patio, Gwen gazed skyward. Stars had replaced the storm clouds. Crossing her arms against the night chill, she inhaled the scent of fresh rain then darted inside.

Then the post-party cleanup began.

Ursula carried leftovers into the kitchen. Tess covered the plates in plastic wrap then stored them in the fridge.

Gwen emptied and washed the witches' cauldron.

Julie filled the dishwasher and set it to run. "Let's call it a night. See you in the morning."

***

Saying goodnight to Tess, Gwen debated about calling Ben, deciding it was now much too late. He wasn't expecting to hear from her anyway. She'd dial his number tomorrow – or would that mislead him about her future intentions for their relationship?

The instant she crawled under the covers, her eyelids began to droop, and she drifted off.

Chapter Twelve

…early morning, Saturday

The next morning, while Tess took her shower, Gwen ventured downstairs. Finding Julie and Ursula in the kitchen, she asked, "Any word from Wyatt about his wife?"

Rummaging through the refrigerated containers, Julie answered, "He hasn't called, so I have no idea."

When distant voices wafted inside, Julie closed the fridge door. "What's that?" Through the living room and out the slider, she paused on the stone patio.

Gwen and Ursula quickly joined her.

"Seems to be coming from the beach," Julie announced, scooting ahead of them. She crossed the lawn and the bluff pathway, stopping on the platform, peering down.

Breathless, Tess came up behind them. "I spotted you three through the guest suite window. What's going on?"

"Don't know yet. We heard voices," Julie answered.

An uncomfortable silence enveloped the four women as they watched the activity far below.

"Those two men in blue uniforms are Nantucket police," Julie advised.

On the steps below, a tall man squatted beside a body caught between the lower railings, his fingers probing the person's neck. When he struggled to his feet and turned, Gwen saw the words 'Medical Examiner' emblazoned on his jacket.

"How horrible," Tess murmured. "Maybe someone washed ashore from a boating accident during the storm?"

Gwen shielded her eyes from the early rays and scanned the shoreline. "I don't see any wreckage." She continued to observe the scene.

The EMTs shifted from one foot to the other as they waited beside their gurney.

A photographer snapped pictures from all angles.

Further away, a balding man spoke to three bystanders: two men and one woman.

When the medical examiner signaled the two EMTs that he was done, they disentangled the body and placed it on their stretcher, then the photographer snapped additional photos.

The sun glinted off the silver in a lone bystander's salt-and-pepper hair as the balding man approached and spoke to him. The man looked up and pointed to the top of the bluff where the four women stood.

Julie stiffened. "Oh, my God. That looks like Wyatt."

Ursula gasped. "Do you suppose the body is his wife?"

"I can't tell from this distance," Julie replied. "The clothing is covered with tidal debris. If that is Wyatt, why did he point up here to us?"

After speaking further to Wyatt, and jotting some notes, the balding man signaled one of the patrolmen and they both hurried along the beach to the north, quickly disappearing beyond the jut of the bluff. In less than a minute, they appeared around the curve of the bluff walk and approached.

The patrolman paused as the balding man stepped toward Julie. "Can I assume you're Ms. Julie Robinson?"

"Yes, that's me," Julie replied. "Have we met?"

"I don't think so." First, he held an official ID close enough for her to read, saying, "Detective Jake Ferguson." Then he thumbed toward the patrolman. "This is Officer Logan Bryce."

Julie studied his badge. "How do you know my name?"

Ferguson waved toward the beach. "The husband of the drowning victim suggested we speak with you."

Julie blanched. "Who was she? Who is he?"

Though Gwen was certain Julie had recognized Wyatt, it never hurt to confirm the facts. Remaining silent, Gwen listened to the exchange without commenting.

The detective's eyes narrowed. "*She* was Sylvia Pierce. *He* is Wyatt Pierce. He says his wife stopped here last night."

Her voice trembling, Julie replied, "That's true. She knocked on my door during our Halloween party."

Detective Ferguson opened his wire-bound notebook and lifted his stubby pencil. "What time was that?"

Shrugging one shoulder, Julie hesitated. "I'd guess eight or even eight-thirty. She didn't stay long."

Detective Ferguson's scribbled her response. "Your phone number, house and email addresses, please."

"Why?" Julie asked.

He glanced at her sideways. "Standard procedure."

After a glance at Ursula to see her cousin nodding, Julie recited the requested specifics.

"We'll also need names, addresses, and phone numbers of the other party guests."

Julie's forehead wrinkled. "Again, why?"

"We'll be taking statements from anyone who may have seen Mrs. Pierce along this stretch of the bluff."

Julie half-turned. "I'll go inside and write down those names for you." She pivoted, scurried across the lawn, and entered via the patio.

While they waited for her return, the detective recorded the contact details for Gwen, Tess, and Ursula.

"Did any of you know Mrs. Pierce?"

Ursula answered first. "I think I can speak for the three of us because we're all weekend guests. We'd never met Mrs. Pierce until last night."

Gwen touched the detective's arm. "What happened?"

He hesitated for only a heartbeat. "It'll be in the local paper this week, so no reason I shouldn't divulge what we know so far. Her death looks like an accidental drowning. We'll know more after the medical examiner provides his report."

The sound of Julie's patio door sliding open silenced everyone as she approached, extending a sheet of paper. "Here's the guest list, Detective."

He folded it and tucked it in his spiral notebook.

"One more question, Ms. Robinson. What was the reason Sylvia Pierce stopped at your place last night?"

Without hesitation, Julie answered, "She was looking for her husband."

"And then Mr. Wyatt arrived later looking for her?"

"That's right," Julie confirmed. "Several of us joined his search, but we never did come across her."

Detective Ferguson snapped his notebook closed. "Thank you all for your cooperation. We'll be in touch if we need additional information."

Nodding, the detective and patrolman reversed their direction on the path and hurried back the way they'd come only minutes earlier.

As they disappeared from view, Julie whispered, "I wonder how Wyatt's holding up."

Chapter Thirteen

… mid-afternoon, Saturday

As Gwen, Ursula, and Tess repacked the outdoor Halloween decorations, Julie appeared on her veranda.

Gwen called over, "Were you able to reach Wyatt?"

"He didn't answer his cell," Julie answered, "so I left a voicemail of condolence."

Just then, a cruiser pulled up the curved driveway and came to a halt near the front walk. Patrolman Bryce emerged and hurried around to open the passenger door.

Detective Ferguson ambled toward them, extending a folded document toward Julie.

"Ms. Robinson, this document is a search warrant for your home, specifically your kitchen."

Obviously confused, Julie unfolded the piece of paper and scanned the words. "You're looking for nutmeg or anything containing nutmeg? What's the meaning of this?" She tossed the warrant onto the walkway.

Gwen wondered the same thing. Even sporadic bakers of homemade goodies maintained a fully stocked pantry of spices, including nutmeg.

The patrolman retrieved the warrant and offered it to Julie a second time.

When she folded her arms, defiantly tucking her hands out of sight, the younger officer placed the warrant atop the nearest box of decorations and stepped aside.

Julie said, "I ask again, what's the meaning of this?"

Detective Ferguson cleared his throat. "I consider you a person of interest in Sylvia Pierce's drowning. Perhaps not directly but involved nevertheless."

"What does nutmeg have to do with anything?" Julie demanded. "You just said she drowned."

"Yes, but it may not have been an accident."

Julie's forehead wrinkled. "What makes you think so?"

"The Cape Cod medical examiner happened to be visiting Nantucket this weekend. His cursory examination of Mrs. Pierce's body on the beach made him suspicious."

"That's interesting," Julie snarled, "but how does finding nutmeg in my kitchen connect me?"

Ferguson kicked a stone from the walkway onto the lawn. "Are you aware, Ms. Robinson, that nutmeg is a hallucinogenic?"

"I am *not* aware of that effect," Julie claimed.

"Patrolman Bryce, let me see your online research," Ferguson commanded.

"Yes, sir," Bryce replied, reaching into his pocket, and handing over a website printout.

Ferguson unfolded the paper, saying, "I want to be accurate, so I'll read this to you."

"Nutmeg contains a psychoactive element called myristicin, whose chemical structure shares similarities with mescaline, amphetamine, and ecstasy, reported to mediate visual, auditory, tactile, and kinesthetic hallucinations, notably the sensation of floating."

"According to your guests, you had sprinkled extra nutmeg onto Mrs. Pierce's eggnog. It could have made her dizzy and caused her to fall down your steps to the beach. When we receive the autopsy findings, we'll know more."

"That's flimsy evidence to consider me a person of interest," Julie argued.

The detective paused. "But there's more. Let's move this conversation to your platform at the top of the bluff."

Julie waved Gwen, Tess, and Ursula to join her.

The four women followed Ferguson around the side of Julie's cottage, with Patrolman Bryce bringing up the rear.

As Julie rounded the oceanside corner of the sunporch, she came to a sudden stop, causing a domino effect as Gwen, Tess, and Ursula bumped into each other.

Righting herself, Gwen leaned to look around Julie.

Crime scene tape surrounded the platform.

Technicians flicked samples into evidence bags.

Julie whirled, her eyes tossing daggers at the detective.

Ignoring her indignation, he said, "There's fresh scuffle marks on that platform. And why didn't you mention Mrs. Pierce's drunken state?"

"That's easy," Julie shot back. "I assumed Wyatt... Mr. Pierce... had already shared her condition with you. I saw no need to besmirch her character any further."

"Then explain this," Ferguson continued. "When you and a few of your guests joined his search last night, why did you discourage them from venturing down these steps?" He pointed at the wooden treads for clarity.

"Because the boards were slippery," Julie snapped.

"But your intention could have been to prevent any of them from shining their flashlights on Mrs. Pierce's body down below after tumbling down those slippery steps."

Julie placed her hands on her hips. "Are you accusing me of pushing her?"

"Well, it's looking like someone did, and you're my most likely suspect."

"Why me?"

"You're the only person who had the means, the motivation, and an opportunity."

"Your assumptions are lame-brained."

"Hang on. Since I spoke to you this morning, we've interviewed your party guests."

Julie instantly retorted, "And what did any of them say that made you decide I was involved?"

Detective Ferguson slowly perused his scribbled notations. "Most of your guests mentioned Mrs. Pierce's accusation that you're having an affair with her husband, Wyatt. Plus, she complained that your excess nutmeg would make her high."

"Wait, wait," Julie began. "If I'd known nutmeg would combine with her drinking and lead to her tragic end, I would never have grated any onto her eggnog. That's flimsy evidence to support any wrongdoing on my part. And, quite frankly, I grated nutmeg on everyone's eggnog. Does that mean I was trying to get all of the people who were at my party high?"

Gwen could sense that Julie was frustrated, and she didn't blame her a bit. The evidence presented so far felt very thin.

"There's more," Ferguson continued. "When Mrs. Pierce requested a private chat with you, you told your guests to retreat to your third-floor studio. You could have guided Mrs. Pierce to this platform and given her a shove."

Detective Ferguson again waved toward the steps leading down to the beach, where evidence techs were packing up their equipment. "She tumbled all the way down until she tangled in the bottom railing. The rise of the storm surge finished her off."

Julie stretched to her full height, her confidence evident. "Your information is incomplete. After I returned from my chat with Sylvia, Nikki went down to convince the woman not to file a complaint about our party noise."

Distracted by the captain's portrait, Gwen hadn't paid much attention to Nikki when she returned from her self-imposed assignment and rejoined them in the studio. The young woman had been very wet from the storm.

If Sylvia had wandered off by herself after Nikki spoke to her, that cleared Julie as the last person to speak to Wyatt's drunken wife.

How about Wyatt himself? His search for Sylvia could have been a charade.

Or as each guest departed, had one of them come upon Sylvia slumped on the platform in a drunken stupor and pushed her down the steps? Gwen again racked her brain to recall who had left via the patio and who by the front door.

Surely no one could have arranged the circumstances ahead of time. The confrontation – if there had been one – had to have been a crime of passion.

Or had Sylvia herself, already drunk and additionally dizzy from the nutmeg, tumbled down the steps accidentally?

More disturbing, had Sylvia chosen suicide as her only option for an unhappy marriage and thrown herself down the slippery surfaces without a push from anyone?

So many possibilities, so little evidence. Multiple potential culprits tripped over one another in Gwen's mind, each vying for the top spot.

Detective Ferguson's voice interrupted Gwen's competing theories when he said, "Hold on a second, Ms. Robinson. Let me find Nikki Quinn's statement."

He handed Julie's list to the patrolman, then returned to his notebook. He paused and scanned the scribbles, clearing his throat before he spoke. "Ms. Quinn didn't answer when we knocked on her door."

"You see?" Julie huffed. "Your so-called reasons to suspect me are non-existent. You have no right to accuse me of any wrong-doing."

The detective's face reddened as he refocused on her. "At the moment, there is insufficient evidence to charge anyone for Mrs. Pierce's death. Do not leave the island until her drowning has been resolved because you remain my top person of interest, Ms. Robinson."

Julie brought her face down to his. "I did not do anything to get rid of Wyatt's wife. He was hired by my contractor for carpentry work in this house. How soon will you wrap this up so I can get on with my life?"

The detective scrubbed his nubbly face. "It's impossible to say. We're short-staffed and will move this investigation along as quickly as we can. We may ask you to come down to the station for further questioning."

Gwen noted the detective's weary expression and stepped up beside Julie. "If I may, sir, you appear exhausted. Many police departments are dealing with staffing issues these days, and I suspect you're working too many hours. If that's the case, may I suggest a possible solution?"

One brow wrinkling, Ferguson countered, "And what would that be... Mrs. Andrews, isn't it?"

"Yes, that's my name, but please call me Gwen."

"In the spirit of civility, what's your suggestion?"

Unsure if she was doing the right thing, Gwen forged ahead. "During the past few years, I've assisted the lead detective in Harbor Falls to resolve several suspicious deaths."

His hands flew into the air. "Thanks, but no thanks, Mrs. Andrews... uh, Gwen. No amateurs allowed."

Gwen shook her head. "You misunderstand. I'm not offering my personal assistance. That lead detective is retired and might be willing to assist you with this investigation."

Assuming that Ben would jump at the chance to revisit Nantucket, Gwen crossed her fingers as she waited for Detective Ferguson's response.

"No one can accuse me of having a closed mind, Gwen." He stopped talking, the wheels in his head obviously spinning. "What's the name of your retired detective?"

While she spelled out *Benjamin Snowcrest*, the detective recorded the name in his notebook. "I'll check his credentials. If everything looks solid, I'll ask my chief to put in a request to the county-wide bureau."

Ferguson turned to the patrolman. "Officer Bryce, we may as well conduct our search for nutmeg."

Both officers headed toward the stone patio.

"Hold on," Julie called after them. "Don't you think your search warrant is a bit premature? Besides, I've already admitted to having nutmeg. Last I knew, that wasn't a crime."

Both officers stopped in their tracks and Ferguson stared at her. "You've made your point. Don't be shocked if we return."

Without another word, the detective and patrolman strode around Julie's cottage toward the front.

The roar of their engine confirmed they had left.

Julie touched Gwen's shoulder. "Thanks for suggesting your detective friend. If he comes over to resolve Sylvia's drowning, tell him he can stay in my studio."

***

"What did you say?" Ben bellowed into Gwen's ear, trying to outshout the cacophony behind him. "Hang on, let me turn down the volume on the football game."

Ben's cell clanged onto an unknown surface. Seconds later, he picked it up. "First of all, it's good to hear from you. Are you and Tess having fun on Nantucket?"

"We were until earlier today," she answered.

"I don't like the sound of that. Are you going to explain, or do you want me to play Twenty Questions?"

Not understanding Ben's snarky remark, Gwen decided he was either anxious to return to his football game, or jealous that she was on Nantucket, and he wasn't.

She forged ahead. "You might get a call to collaborate with Detective Ferguson of the Nantucket police."

For several seconds Ben didn't speak. "That's not at all what I expected you to say. Did he request my services?"

"Not yet. Their department is short-staffed, so I mentioned that you might be willing to lend them a hand."

"Well, this won't be the first time for intra-county cooperation, but this is a first from Nantucket."

"I'm sorry if I overstepped, Ben. I thought you'd welcome an excuse to escape Harbor Falls for a while."

When Ben said nothing, Gwen hurried to fill the void. "Will this interfere with your Sunday afternoon concert tickets?"

She pictured his white hair swaying as he shook his head. "Not at all. I already gave away those tickets."

"Then why are you hesitating? I thought you'd jump at the chance to revisit Nantucket."

Ben harrumphed. "Sorry for being short with you, Gwen. What's your opinion of this Detective Ferguson's openness to another investigator?"

Relieved, Gwen answered, "He seemed interested because he's exhausted. What I haven't told you is that he suspects Tess's college roommate was involved in a woman's death."

After a pause, Ben reacted. "And you're thinking I can prove Tess's roommate innocent?"

"Tess and I both hope so. We can't imagine Julie had anything to do with that woman's drowning."

"Any chance the drowning was an accident?"

"That's one of my theories."

When Ben didn't ask why, Gwen forged ahead. "Detective Ferguson is checking your credentials before he asks his chief to put in the request for your services."

"In that case, I'll have to wait until I hear from someone official. I'll let you know what happens."

When he disconnected the call, Gwen roamed Julie's guest suite, stopping at the window. She stared at the platform, wondering the real reason Sylvia had died.

Mesmerized by the restless ocean waves, she settled on the window seat, losing track of time until her cell buzzed. Ben.

"Good news, Gwen. Just received the official request for my consulting services. I bought my ticket for the early ferry that docks at ten tomorrow morning."

"That's the same boat Tess and I rode yesterday. I'll ask Julie to drive us into town and meet you at the dock. She said to mention you can sleep in her studio daybed."

"Hold on," Ben protested. "If Julie is a person of interest, I can't accept any favors from her. I'll rent my own car and book my own lodging."

"You're right, Ben. The conflict of interest should have occurred to me."

"No reason it would." He hesitated. "Listen, Gwen, I apologize for my sharpness when you called earlier. The football game was tied, and my favorite team was about to kick a field goal for the win. Then it occurred to me that I could rewind. Can you forgive me?"

"Of course," she answered. She'd forgive her treasured friend Ben for just about anything.

"Thanks," he said. "I can't wait to tell our police chief that I'll be out of town until further notice. After I'm settled tomorrow, I'll call you."

As he disconnected the call, Gwen's original plan to return to Harbor Falls late Sunday or early Monday popped into her head. Assuming she'd be staying on the island for unknown extra days, she needed to arrange the care and feeding of her cat, Amber.

Retrieving her phone, she texted both Liz and Jenna with no idea how quickly either of them would respond.

Chapter Fourteen

… early morning, Sunday

Minutes before ten, the fast ferry slowed to a crawl as it approached the dock. Because Ben had wandered to a less crowded section on the upper deck, he disembarked with the last of the passengers, a talkative couple visiting their daughter and teenaged grandchildren.

As the throng of greeters thinned to a trickle, a policeman with a crew cut and serious expression waved to Ben.

"Officer Bryce?" Ben asked as he approached.

"Yes, sir, but please call me Logan. We tend to be less formal out here."

"If we're going to be informal, call me Ben."

"All right, Ben. Pleasant crossing?"

"A brief squall. My jacket's already dry."

"Can I help you with your luggage?"

"No, no," Ben answered, extending the wand of his wheeled pullman. "I've got it."

Crossing the uneven dock boards, Ben kept pace with the younger officer.

Buckling into the passenger seat of the cruiser, he glanced at Logan. "Is Detective Ferguson meeting with me today?"

Logan nodded. "I'm driving you directly to the station."

As the landscape whizzed by, Ben recalled his long-ago honeymoon with his long-divorced wife. After all the years between, nothing looked familiar. But then, he'd had no need to find the police station during that first trip.

Logan pulled into the parking lot fronting the brick station. As he led Ben toward the entrance, three people scooted inside ahead of them.

"Busy place," Ben commented.

"That's because this building offers community rooms where groups can schedule their meetings."

Logan led the way up the stairs and along the hallway until he knocked on the frame of an open door.

Behind the desk, an older man pushed himself to his feet, his hand extended. "I'm Detective Jake Ferguson. You must be Detective Benjamin Snowcrest. Welcome to Nantucket."

Ben returned the handshake.

Ferguson eased himself down into his chair. "I'm glad you're willing to lend us a hand." He waved toward the visitors' chairs. "Have a seat."

Before sitting, Ben glanced at the multiple commendations framed and mounted on the walls.

Lingering within the open door, Logan asked, "Want me to stay, sir?"

Ben picked up that the patrolman, though less formal with some, deferred to Ferguson's status.

Ferguson indicated the empty second chair. "Yes."

Logan sat, leaning forward, revealing his enthusiasm.

81

Ferguson folded his hands atop his blotter. "Patrolman Bryce is interested in joining our detective squad, so I'm assigning him to assist you during your investigation."

Ben nodded but refrained from commenting about being saddled with an inexperienced wannabe.

Switching his focus, Ferguson said, "I researched your record of arrests, Ben. Impressive."

"Thanks. Some people are born with a nose for chasing clues. I just happen to be one of them."

"Well put. Gwen Andrews holds you in high regard. I'm glad she suggested bringing you over. Have you been to Nantucket before?"

"Haven't made the trip since my honeymoon, so I'm grateful for this opportunity to revisit."

"Did you leave your wife back in Harbor Falls?"

Shaking his head, Ben said, "We divorced years ago. She couldn't live with the constant stress of marriage to a law enforcement officer."

"That's unfortunate," Ferguson commented while opening a file folder. A small notebook tumbled out, which Ferguson pushed aside before fanning the other documents across his blotter. "Let me explain the case."

Examining each piece one by one, they discussed the summary sheet of basic details, the multiple photos of Sylvia Pierce's body, the coroner's preliminary report, a hand-written list of party guests' names and addresses, ending with a website printout about nutmeg.

Ferguson picked up the errant notebook and waved it. "This contains my initial interviews on the beach plus Ms. Robinson and her three houseguests yesterday morning. Then the statements from her party guests, ending with my afternoon return to Ms. Robinson's home for follow-up."

Flipping page by page, he summarized each interview, ending with Julie's criticism of Nikki's missing statement. He reached into his bottom desk drawer and removed a new notebook. "Here's a fresh one if you fill this one."

Ben considered the lack of evidence. "What makes you so suspicious of Julie Robinson?"

"First, let me explain why I jumped at Mrs. Andrews' … uh, Gwen's… suggestion to request your expertise. First, we're short-staffed. Plus my wife is… was… a friend to Sylvia Pierce. They've planned dinners with me and Wyatt Pierce. I need to distance myself or risk an accusation of favoritism."

"Understandable," Ben murmured.

"Now I'll answer your question about my suspicion of Julie Robinson. Wyatt was hired during the renovation of Ms. Robinson's cottage, so the two of them spent quite a bit of time together. Sylvia often complained to my wife that they were having an affair. During the Halloween party, Sylvia accused Julie in front of her guests."

"Embarrassment as motivation?" Ben asked.

"That and the chance to free Wyatt from his marriage. The storm provided the opportunity, though forensics has yet to provide evidence."

Ben reacted. "And those are the reasons you suspect Ms. Robinson of pushing Mrs. Pierce down those steps?"

"Exactly," Ferguson said. "Ability, opportunity, and motivation all wrapped in the lovely package of Ms. Julie Robinson."

When Ben stretched his hand toward the notebook, Detective Ferguson placed it in his palm. Reading through the pages, Ben paused. "Have you confirmed that Wyatt was attending the Al-Anon meeting that evening?"

"Not yet," Ferguson answered. "But unless Wyatt has become a very convincing actor, he appeared genuinely upset when he identified Sylvia's body after that beach walker reported it."

When Ben started to react, Ferguson held up his hand.

"I know what you're going to say. The husband is usually the prime suspect. As the independent investigator, it's now your job to determine if Wyatt is innocent."

Ferguson slumped in his chair, his exhaustion obvious.

Ben held up the notebook. "This stays in the case file?"

"It does." Ferguson reached into his desk drawer and offered two more notebooks. "In case you fill the one I already gave you. Do you have any questions?"

"Not yet. I need to interview a few people. You know how this works… one conversation leads to another."

Shoving the sparse evidence into the folder, Ferguson pushed the file across his desk.

Ben reached for it. "I'd like to begin with your wife."

"Yes, yes, of course." Ferguson grabbed a pencil, jotting an address and phone number on a sticky note. "Call first to be sure she's home. My wife is involved in community projects."

Detective Ferguson indicated Logan. "Patrolman Bryce can drive you to my house whenever you're ready."

"Thanks, but I'd rather have my own car. Which rental company do you recommend?"

Ferguson waved his hand in dismissal. "No need. I'll assign an unmarked sedan for your use. Have you booked a room?"

"Not yet. I refused Ms. Robinson's offer of lodging."

"Smart of you to avoid a conflict of interest while you're investigating the lady."

"I'm investigating everyone," Ben corrected.

Ferguson grunted and lifted his phone. "Give me a sec to make a quick call." After less than a minute of conversation, Ferguson covered the receiver. "My sister-in-law owns a small guest house. Her current guests checked out early and left on the ferry, so she has a vacant room. Interested?"

At Ben's nod, Ferguson confirmed and disconnected. He ripped off a second sticky note and jotted the name and address of the guest house.

Ben affixed both sticky notes to the inside flap of the case folder. "I appreciate you making that request."

"Ulterior motive. I'll know where you're staying if I need to see you after hours. And don't worry about the cost, Maeve will bill the department directly. Thanks again for making the trip, Ben. Keep me posted."

85

When Logan stood up, he asked, "Do you want me to arrange the unmarked car?"

"You do that, Patrolman Bryce."

Logan stopped at the door, obviously waiting for Ben to follow him.

Noticing Ben's reluctance, Ferguson said, "He'll meet you out back in a few minutes."

When Logan's footsteps faded down the hallway, Ferguson turned to Ben. "Is there something else?"

"There is. It concerns Gwen Andrews."

His expression curious, Ferguson sat back down. "I've been wondering about your relationship with her."

"Gwen's behind the scenes sleuthing helped me solve several cases. I'd like her to be my Confidential Informant."

Ferguson half-swiveled his chair and stared out his window, finally turning back to Ben. "We rarely allow civilians to get involved. What would she contribute?"

"She's met the guests who attended the Halloween party and has an uncanny way of speaking to people without them suspecting she's investigating. Even if none of the guests pushed Mrs. Pierce, they might connect Gwen with others who held a grudge against the woman."

"Well," Ferguson reacted, drawing out the word. "All right. Bring her in to sign a C.I. agreement."

Ben got to his feet. "Which way to the back lot?"

As they strode the winding hallways to a door at the rear of the building, Ferguson repeated, "Keep me posted."

86

In the back parking lot, Logan stood at the open door of a sedan, holding out a business card. "My personal cell number is on the back. Let me know if you need any department resources. I've transferred your suitcase to the trunk."

"Thank you, Logan."

Though Ben appreciated the patrolman's enthusiasm, he stopped short of making any promises. On the other hand, with no idea of the roadblocks he might encounter, Ben assumed Logan might indeed become useful.

Tucking the card in his pocket, Ben sensed disappointment in Logan, so said, "Thanks for picking me up at the dock and driving me to the station. I'll text you."

Chapter Fifteen

… late morning, Sunday

After typing the guest house address into the onboard GPS, Ben exited the police lot and steered toward town. He soon spotted the inn's sign on the front lawn and parked in a small lot beside a saltbox-style house.

As he approached the front entrance, the contrast of the grey weathered shingles against yellow, purple, and orange flowers brought Gwen to mind. With each season, she embellished her home in a similar fashion.

How soon and how often would he have a chance to see Gwen during his time on Nantucket? Would she agree to reprise her role as his C.I., or would she turn him down, preferring to devote her time to Julie Robinson?

When Ben rapped on the blue door, a woman's voice called from inside, "Come in, it's unlocked."

A bit surprised she didn't first look through the sidelights to check who was knocking, he remembered that Jake had called her, so she was expecting a new boarder.

As he pushed the door inward, a petite woman hustled down the hallway, her hand extended. "You must be Ben Snowcrest. My name is Maeve. Welcome to my guest house. Will you be wantin' lunch today?"

Her Irish accent charming, Ben hesitated.

And then his stomach rumbled. "Sounds like I'm hungry, so, yes, thank you."

"First, let me show you to your room."

An idea popped into Ben's mind. "Before you do, may I invite a friend who is also visiting Nantucket? I'd be happy to pay for her meal."

Maeve waved off his offer. "No need. I made a pot of Irish stew. There's plenty. Let me know when she'll be joinin' you, and I'll set the table for two."

***

When Gwen saw Ben's name appear on her caller ID, she carried her cell phone out to the stone patio. "Any problems during your ferry ride, Ben?"

"Only a short squall. A patrolman met me at the docks and drove me to the police station. Detective Ferguson reviewed the few details of the case."

"Where are you now?"

"At a guest house in town. But listen, Gwen, let's not discuss this on the phone. If you haven't eaten lunch, can you join me? I can pick you up."

"You already have a rental?"

"Not a rental. Ferguson assigned an unmarked police sedan for me to drive during the investigation."

"That's great. Yes, I'd enjoy lunch with you. We can talk about the case."

"Wonderful. What's Julie's address?"

Gwen listened as his pencil scratched the number and street until he said, "After I get settled into my room here, I'll head your way. See you soon." Ben disconnected.

When Gwen retreated into the cottage, Tess, Julie, and Ursula all stared at her.

Tess was the first to speak. "Was that Ben?"

"Yes. He'll be picking me up for lunch."

"Do we get to meet your detective friend?" Julie asked.

Gwen shrugged one shoulder. "I'm sure you will at some point. But I have no idea when that will happen."

"Well, tell him I'm anxious to speak with him."

"I'll do that." Gwen swiveled toward the staircase. "I'm going to change and then wait out front for Ben."

"Just like in high school?" Tess teased.

Flicking her hand toward her sister, Gwen headed upstairs. Thinking she'd only be on Nantucket for the weekend, she hadn't packed many clothes, but she'd surely brought something suitable.

***

Stopping at the door to Maeve's kitchen, Ben said, "My friend has agreed to join me for lunch. I'd like to freshen up if you can show me to my room."

"Certainly. Right this way." She led him up the narrow stairs to the first room at the front of the house. "You have a private bath. If you want fresh towels, leave your wet ones on the bathroom floor. I'll be downstairs if you need anything before you leave to pick up your friend."

After thanking her, Ben hung his shirts and slacks in the closet, his unmentionables in the dresser drawers. Bounding down the stairs, he poked his head into the kitchen.

"I'll be back soon, Maeve. Your stew smells delicious."

Settled into the car, Ben punched Julie's address into his GPS, then turned the key and followed its directions.

Turning into the curved driveway, he glimpsed Julie's house, muttering, *'Nice'* as he parked at the end of the front walkway. When Gwen descended the veranda steps, he reached sideways to push open the passenger door.

She leaned in, her expression wary. "Hi, Ben. Julie asked if she'd meet you when you arrive."

Unprepared for a chat with Ferguson's person of interest, Ben said, "Maybe when I bring you back."

He glanced at the veranda, relieved Julie wasn't standing there, staring at him. "You ready for lunch?"

Gwen nodded as she settled in the passenger seat, then closed the door, and buckled herself in. "Let's go."

***

Content to be sitting in Ben's passenger seat, Gwen said, "I'm glad you agreed to take this case."

"I wasn't about to refuse. Thanks again for recommending me to Detective Ferguson."

"He appeared overwhelmed. It made sense to suggest that he ask for your assistance."

Ben steered along the main road toward town. "Until I stepped off the ferry, I didn't realize how much I've always wanted to revisit Nantucket. I doubt I'll have a chance to be a tourist, but at least I'm here." He tossed her a wan smile. "With your help of course."

Gwen half-joked, "Where would you be without me?"

"Funny lady," he quipped. "Most likely chasing another criminal for Chief Brown back in Harbor Falls

As they passed the cookie cutter development, Gwen waved toward it. "Sections of the island are still charming, but the modern world has invaded."

Ben glanced to where she was pointing. "Everyone needs a roof over their head." His tone turned serious. "I'm aware you and Tess hope I can eliminate Julie as a suspect, but I can't make any promises. I have to let the evidence tell the story."

"I'm aware of that, Ben. All you can do is chase the clues until you figure out how Sylvia Pierce ended up at the bottom of those slippery wooden steps."

"She could have stumbled without anyone's help."

"I'm glad to hear you say that," Gwen commented. "Sylvia was either pushed or stumbled on her own."

"Too early to hazard a guess," Ben said. "But now that we're discussing her death, are you interested in resurrecting your role as my C.I. for this case?"

The possibility of once again sleuthing behind the scenes for Ben increased Gwen's heart rate. "Does Nantucket allow our type of arrangement?"

Ben refocused on the road. "Reluctantly. After Ferguson shared the details of the drowning, I mentioned our previous collaborations and he was open to the idea. If you agree, we need to stop by his office for you to sign a C.I. agreement. We can do that after lunch, before I return you to Julie's house. If you agree, that is."

"Of course I agree, Ben. My behind the scenes sleuthing combined with your official investigation will hopefully uncover the details of Sylvia's death and remove Julie as Ferguson's person of interest."

Ben reached over and squeezed Gwen's hand. "Your attitude is exactly why I like you as my partner."

Gwen didn't miss his subtle hint that he'd also like her to be his life partner. "Just give me a sec to check with Tess about our ferry tickets."

Within a minute, she'd dialed, asked the question, listened to Tess's response, and disconnected.

"Tess wants to remain on Nantucket to support Julie. She'll call the ferry service and rebook our tickets to an open-ended return. If Julie's expecting other guests this week, Tess and I will find other lodging."

She observed the homes and businesses as Ben maneuvered the narrow streets of Nantucket, finally pulling up to a charming guest house.

"Here we are, Gwen. My temporary home sweet home. Maeve is serving our lunch."

"Sweet," Gwen commented, undoing her seat belt.

Ben hurried around and opened her door. "If you and Tess aren't able to stay with Julie, Maeve might have extra rooms."

"That's a good Plan B but I am guessing I'll be most useful to you if I can remain at Julie's cottage."

Ben led the way up the steps and knocked on the blue door.

The door opened and a petite woman said, "Welcome back, Mr. Snowcrest. You don't need to knock. I expect my guests to come and go."

Introductions completed, Maeve waved toward the dining room. "Make yourselves comfortable. There's a pot of Irish tea steepin' on the table. I'll be right back with your lunch."

As they savored the delicious stew and fresh baked rolls, he glanced toward the kitchen and lowered his voice. "I need to show you the case file that Ferguson handed me, but not here."

In that instant, Gwen came to a decision. With no intention of ruining her working relationship with Ben, she'd avoid the charged subject of their conflicting personal expectations. She knew well that Ben wanted more than a peck on her cheek or a squeeze of her hand.

Her vivid imagination taking over, she wondered about Ben's reaction when she explained why they could never become a real couple. Would he remain in her life or abandon their friendship? She'd broach that dreaded conversation after they both returned to Harbor Falls.

Maeve walked in. "Would either of you like a second helping of anything?"

Ben patted his stomach. "That was delicious, but I can't eat another spoonful."

"Neither can I," Gwen said. "You're a good cook, Maeve."

The innkeeper blushed. "Thank you. I pride myself on my cooking skills and strive to keep my guests satisfied."

"Mission accomplished," Ben acknowledged. "Do you happen to have a copy machine? I need only a dozen pages."

She pointed across the hall. "It's in the corner of the sitting room. Help yourself."

Chapter Sixteen

… mid-afternoon, Sunday

Gwen turned from watching the scenery and noticed Ben pulling into the police station. "Why are we stopping here?"

"Did you forget about signing the C.I. agreement?"

Her face warmed. "I did forget... sorry."

They entered the lobby and approached the enclosed reception desk. A female officer slid open the window. "Can I help you?"

"Yes. My name is Benjamin Snowcrest, and this is Gwen Andrews. Detective Ferguson is expecting us."

The woman picked up the phone. "Hold on. I'll check to make sure he's available." After a brief conversation, she said, "Detective Ferguson will be down in a minute."

While they waited, Ben inspected the framed maps, artwork, and island photos that hung on the walls while Gwen scanned community flyers.

The elevator doors opened, and Detective Ferguson hurried into the lobby. "You're back, Ben. And Mrs. Andrews... uh, Gwen, good to see you again. This way."

He waved them into the elevator, and they exited on the second floor. After they were seated in his office, Ferguson pulled a form from his bottom drawer and handed it to Gwen.

"Ben mentioned you've acted as his C.I. before, but if you have any questions before you sign, just ask."

After Gwen reviewed the terms, she filled in the required details and dashed off her signature on the dotted line before sliding the document back to him.

Ferguson gave the form a cursory glance, then locked it away in his desk drawer. "We go to great lengths, Gwen, to keep your status confidential. Be sure you do the same."

Then he turned to Ben. "My wife just called to say she'll be busy with church activities this afternoon but more available to speak with you tomorrow."

"Then I'll call her in the morning," Ben said.

Ferguson stood and extended his hand first to Gwen and then to Ben. "I appreciate the two of you helping with the Sylvia Pierce investigation."

A knock on the open doorframe.

Patrolman Bryce ducked as he entered. "Sorry to interrupt, sir, but the coroner called. His final autopsy report won't be ready for a few more days."

"Damn," Ferguson swore under his breath. "I was counting on him to resolve questions about the drowning."

A second knock drew their attention.

within the same doorframe, a different officer paused. "Detective Ferguson, we need you down the hall, sir."

Getting to his feet, Ferguson extended his hand to Ben. "Officer Bryce will escort you and Gwen to the lobby. Stay in touch, Ben. We'll talk soon."

Foregoing the elevator, the young patrolman led them down the front stairs and held open the door to the front parking lot.

***

As they walked toward Ben's loaner, Gwen inhaled the distinctive scent of autumn leaves, hoping the aroma would calm her nerves. Adrenalin surged through her body as she embarked on an investigation with no idea of the outcome.

To feel normal, she commented, "Busy police department."

"Seems to be," Ben replied. "I'd guess Ferguson's working seven days a week. You'd think an island doesn't see much crime, but criminals never take a vacation. Thanks again for suggesting me to him."

"Like I told you before, the man looked exhausted, and I thought you wouldn't mind escaping Harbor Falls for a while. Do you want to go over the case file before you drop me back at Julie's house?"

Although Ben nodded, he glanced up at another group of people entering the station and started the engine. "Yes to your question, but let's find a little more privacy."

Relocating to a deserted side lot, Ben backed the sedan into a secluded parking spot that provided a view of cars entering and leaving the station.

He reached into the back seat, jostled a shopping bag, then held out a journal with a tapestry cover. "I bought this for you to record your activities."

Stroking the cover, Gwen said, "Thanks, Ben, this will come in handy. Plus, it's beautiful." She flipped to the first blank page, noting the date and time, then glanced over at him, pen poised. "I'm ready to hear the details."

Ben again stretched to the back seat, pulling forward his briefcase, which he balanced on the console.

As Ben sifted through the contents, Gwen snuck a side glance at his profile. Despite his years and white hair, he projected a masculine confidence that was hard to ignore.

Gwen had forgiven *herself* for responding to his intense kiss back in June. But would *Ben* forgive her for misleading him, albeit impulsively? She so wanted to remain his friend, but that's as far as she could ever let their connection progress.

Surely there were women who'd jump at the chance to date Ben and satisfy his longing for romance.

When an object slid from Ben's folder, it jolted Gwen from her musings. She grabbed the small spiral notebook before it hit the floorboards. "Is this Ferguson's?"

"Yep," Ben answered. "He also assigned Patrolman Bryce to assist if I need anything from the department."

"Will you call on him?"

"Hard to say. At this point, I have no idea what information we might need that I can't access on my own. Apparently Bryce is hoping to move into the detective unit, but I didn't plan on supervising a rookie during this investigation. I'm avoiding that situation as much as possible."

Ben removed several documents and stared.

Leaning around the edge of his open briefcase, Gwen saw that he was gaping at photographs.

When she stretched out her hand, expecting him to pass them over, he angled the pictures away from her view, saying, "You don't want to see these."

"Why not? They have to do with the case, don't they?"

"Yes, but they're disturbing."

She wiggled the fingers of her outstretched hand. "If I'm going to help you, Ben, I need to see everything. I can handle whatever those photos are showing."

"All right, but remember I warned you." He held out the three photographs.

Gwen positioned them in the light streaming through her passenger window. For a moment, she couldn't speak.

And then she murmured, "Sylvia's body?"

"Yes. Caught in the beach step railings." Ben's voice took on an almost reverent tone. "That's where a young woman came upon Sylvia early Saturday morning."

"A woman?" Gwen said, startled. "I thought her husband found her. Wyatt Pierce was at the scene when Julie, Ursula, Tess, and I came outside to check on the voices we'd heard. We were watching from the top of the bluff when Wyatt pointed at us for Detective Ferguson."

"Maybe so, but he wasn't the one who found Sylvia."

Gwen scanned the photos one more time, studying the details despite the disturbing graphic reality of Sylvia's death. "You're right, Ben. These pictures are quite unsettling."

Gently prying them from Gwen's fingers, he slid the photos behind the other documents, then passed over several sheets.

"These are copies of the party guest statements. After you've chatted with each of them, I'll be interested to hear your gut instincts about their involvement... or not... in Sylvia Pierce's death."

Gwen paged through the statements, skimming the words. "I'll study these more closely before I meet with each one."

Ben handed over another piece of paper. "Here's a photocopy of the guest list Julie created for Detective Ferguson with addresses and phone numbers. Any idea how you'll approach her friends?"

"I've been contemplating that myself. In Harbor Falls, I knew the potential suspects. But out here on Nantucket, I only just met these women at Julie's party. Even if they know about Sylvia's drowning due to Detective Ferguson's questioning on Saturday morning, they may not be aware that Julie is his primary person of interest. I'll need to find excuses to run into each of them. Updating each guest about the police interest in Julie will give me a reason to begin a conversation."

"That's a perfect segue," Ben agreed.

Gwen ran her finger down the list. "I see that Crystal lives on Baxter Road, north of Julie's cottage. I overheard her telling another party guest that she walks on the beach with her kids, but I have no idea of her schedule. This afternoon, I'll take a stroll in that direction. With any luck, I'll bump into her."

"Good idea. Do you remember what she looks like?"

"I think so." Gwen's mind brought forth the image of a petite blonde.

Ben's voice jostled the memory. "Here's a different question about opportunity. After the party, did each friend leave by herself, or with another guest?"

Gwen's mind whizzed back to Friday night. "One at a time. I'd have to concentrate on who exited across the patio and who went out the front door. Why is that important?"

After reviewing the coroner's preliminary report and the nutmeg printout, Ben nudged all the documents into a neat pile. "If someone fought with Sylvia on that platform, we need to find a witness."

"And you think Julie's guests might have seen someone when they left the party," Gwen stated rather than asked. "That would assume Sylvia was on that platform long after she interrupted Julie's party. And wouldn't that guest have mentioned seeing another person when Ferguson questioned all of them on Saturday morning?"

"Based on their statements, it appears he was only gathering witness accounts of Sylvia barging through Julie's door the night before."

Folding her set of statements in half, Gwen tucked them at the back of the journal, "So, at that point, he wasn't suspicious about the way Sylvia died."

"That's my hunch. That's why it'll be helpful if you chat with each of them. In addition to spotting Sylvia on that platform, they might share local gossip about Sylvia and possibly Julie that they wouldn't share with the police."

"We won't know if they have anything to tell until I begin

my sleuthing. When will you interview Julie?"

"This afternoon if possible," Ben replied. "Tomorrow morning, I'll hopefully interview Ferguson's wife."

"Why his wife?" Gwen asked, tucking the tapestry journal with photocopies into her tote bag.

Ben reopened the front flap of the case file and tapped the top sticky note. "Ferguson's wife Addie was friends with Sylvia Pierce. The two couples got together on a regular basis. That's Ferguson's second reason to hand off the investigation to a third party, which is me."

"But why interview Addie?"

"Because Sylvia had been complaining about an affair between Wyatt and Julie." Ben slid the folder into his briefcase and snapped the lock before tossing it into the back seat.

"Addie," he continued, "hounded Ferguson to check into Sylvia's drowning. He realized his personal involvement was a conflict of interest because he wouldn't want to suspect his friend Wyatt. In fact, Ferguson already said as much."

"Then it's a good thing you accepted his offer."

"I predict this investigation will reveal a few surprises for everyone," Ben said, lifting one eyebrow.

"That remains to be seen," Gwen retorted.

"Okay, here's our plan. At the end of each day, call me when Julie is out of earshot so we can compare notes. Per the Confidential Informant Agreement, it's best if she never finds out you're working behind the scenes for me."

"I'm aware of the boundaries, Ben."

He grinned at her. "Just checking. Right now, I'd better take you back to Julie's cottage. On the way, tell me your impressions of Tess's college roommate and how likely that she was involved in Sylvia Pierce's demise."

Chapter Seventeen
… mid-afternoon, Sunday

After parking in front of Julie's cottage, Ben walked beside Gwen until they reached the veranda.

The front door flew open, and an attractive woman posed in the opening. "Welcome back, you two."

She extended her hand. "Julie Robinson."

He returned her handshake. "Ben Snowcrest."

"Nice to meet you. Please come in." She waved them into the foyer, where Ben noticed Gwen's sister standing beside another woman with raven black hair.

"Hi, Tess," Ben greeted.

Julie came up beside him. "And this is Ursula, my cousin visiting from Vermont."

Ben reached for the woman's outstretched bejeweled fingers, discerning no family resemblance. "Hello."

"I hope you can stay for a while," Julie urged.

"Thanks, but bringing Gwen back here is the extent of my social call. You no doubt are aware I've been asked to investigate the drowning of Sylvia Pierce. Is there a place where I can speak with each of you separately?"

Ben's jacket flapped open.

Julie side-stepped. "You carry a gun?"

He quickly covered the weapon. "Yes, I do. Sorry if it startled you."

"I hate guns," she muttered, then pointed toward the wide staircase. "My studio on the third floor is quite private. We can talk up there."

As Ben followed her up the first flight, Gwen, Tess, and Ursula scattered in three different directions.

Reaching the third floor, Julie slid open a frosted door and moved to the side, waving him in.

Ben noticed an easel angled in such a way to catch the light from the front windows and the skylight above. "You're a painter, Ms. Robinson?"

"Let's not be so formal. Please call me Julie." She reached for a brush and stared at it. I haven't put paint to canvas since college art classes. After this Sylvia nonsense is over, I'll try my hand at a seascape."

Hoping Julie was right – about both her revived artist skills and the resolution of Mrs. Pierce's drowning – Ben shifted his briefcase to his other hand. "Your home is quite charming."

"Thanks," she responded. "This cottage was overdue for some TLC, which lowered the price."

"Was this studio already here?"

She shook her head, "No. This space was a dusty attic, filled with old furniture and pictures. My carpenter transported usable items to a consignment shop. Then swept the dirt before he began his transformation. May I show you a treasured find?"

Ben tore his attention from his surroundings. "Sure."

Julie led him to the far end where a daybed and several chairs formed a conversation area and pointed toward the portrait hanging on the wall,

Ben studied the man's solemn face. "Who's he?"

"Captain Percy Tiffin," Julie answered, a note of pride in her voice. "He built this house in the mid-1800s." For a long moment, she gazed at the sea captain's likeness. Turning from the painting, her dark blue eyes peered into Ben's as she asked, "Do you believe in ghosts?"

Taken aback by her question, he paused. Not wanting to delay his interview with a side discussion about the paranormal, he resisted the urge to tell her about his encounter with the ghost that haunted the Harbor Falls B&B. And months later, his chat with the ghost of Gwen's husband.

To Julie, he said, "That's an unusual question to ask someone you just met. Let's just say I have an open mind."

She sat in a side chair. "I've heard stories that my Captain – and I've come to think of him as mine – is rumored to wander this house, but I've never seen him. My cousin Ursula came over this weekend to attempt a connection."

To be polite, Ben asked, "How will she do that?"

"Ursula's a medium. During our séance at the Halloween party, she attempted to summon the captain."

Another bit of unexpected news. Given Gwen's link to her husband's ghost, he was surprised she hadn't mentioned the attempt to communicate with Julie's captain. "A séance?"

"Yes," Julie confirmed. "Unfortunately, Captain Tiffin didn't join us. I was quite disappointed. We're attempting a second séance this evening. Would you like to stay?"

Ben found her invitation a bit unsettling as he responded. "Under normal circumstances, I would, but I need to avoid a conflict of interest while I'm investigating Sylvia Pierce's drowning." Ben rested his briefcase on the low table in front of him and snapped open the locks to refocus on his reason for being there.

Briefly closing her eyes, Julie leaned back. "Too bad."

Ben had previously reread the two interviews with Julie in Ferguson's official notebook, so turned now to the next blank page, his pencil poised to record her answers. "Your carpenter was Sylvia Pierce's husband?"

Julie sat upright and stiffened. "That's right. His work ended about a month ago."

"But his wife thought she'd find him here on Friday night?"

"I told Sylvia he wasn't here. She didn't stay long."

"But she stayed long enough for you to serve her eggnog?" He located the website printout. "I never heard of nutmeg dizziness."

"Neither had I, Ben. May I call you Ben?"

When he nodded, she continued. "If I'd had any idea…" her words trailed off.

Ben scribbled. "Mrs. Pierce asked to speak in private?"

"That's right. So I wouldn't inconvenience my guests, I suggested they gather up here and wait for me."

He flipped through the statements from the other women, pausing once in a while to read before continuing. "And when you rejoined your guests, you told them Mrs. Pierce accused you of having an affair with her husband?"

"She had actually accused me of being a 'slut' in front of my guests. When I returned from speaking with her, they asked me why she wanted to talk to me."

Ben scribbled her reply.

"Had you become friends with Wyatt Pierce?"

"More acquaintances than friends," Julie insisted, her tone irritated. "I met Wyatt after my contractor hired him to create this studio." She waved to include every facet of the space. "You can see what a fine craftsman he is."

Using an age-old interview tactic, Ben paused and waited for Julie to fill the silence. He wasn't disappointed.

"Detective," she began, "… Ben. Has anyone told you that Sylvia was a raging alcoholic? She'd accused one of my party guests of having an affair with Wyatt during her kitchen update project. This isn't her first bout with false accusations."

Ben located the statement. "Yes, I see Evie mentioned it during her initial interview. Besides the two of you, did Mrs. Pierce accuse anyone else?"

Julie shrugged. "You'll have to ask Wyatt."

Ben switched gears. "Can you point out the place where she began her fall to the beach?"

Getting to her feet, Julie waved him to the closest dormer window and pointed down.

Ben studied the bird's eye view. Beyond the shallow lawn and a dirt path sat a wooden platform. Crime-scene tape no longer isolated the site of a probable – but as-yet-unproved – crime. As Gwen had indicated during their lunch, with the storm raging on Friday night, Sylvia could have slipped on the wet boards and fallen to her death without assistance from anyone else.

Julie's whisper interrupted Ben's analysis.

"Detective Ferguson thinks I purposely shoved Sylvia from that platform."

Softening his own voice, Ben pushed. "Other than grating nutmeg on Sylvia's eggnog, *were* you involved?"

Though her volume didn't increase, Julie gritted her teeth, simmering like a riptide beneath the surface. "Ferguson asked me that. I told him I wasn't."

Ben needed to be more specific. "But *did* you have an affair with Wyatt Pierce?"

Her skin blanching, Julie glared at Ben. "I divorced my second husband, bought this house, and relocated my life from North Carolina. I'm not in the market for a man."

Ben noted that she'd danced around his questions, but he wasn't prepared to guess why or aggravate her any further at this early stage of his investigation. He remained undecided about her guilt... or innocence.

***

After Ben and Julie headed up the staircase, Gwen had said to Tess and Ursula, "If you'll excuse me, I need to make some phone calls." Retreating to the sunroom, she tapped the number of Fiction 'n Fables Bookstop.

Liz answered on the third ring. "Hi, Gwen. You calling to tell me which ferry you're riding from Nantucket?"

"Didn't you get my text yesterday?"

"Don't think so. Let me double check." A second later, Liz said. "No text from you. What was your message?"

Annoyed at the spotty cell reception, Gwen answered. "There's been a tragedy out here." She explained Sylvia's drowning and Julie's status as a person of interest.

"How awful," Liz said. "What happens now?"

"At my suggestion, Ben rode the ferry over this morning to investigate the case. Tess and I will be staying to support Julie while she deals with this."

"Completely understandable," Liz murmured.

"I have no idea how long I'll stay on Nantucket. Could you stop over at my house tonight to feed Amber? I'll try to catch up with Jenna and find out when she's returning from her Vermont trip to take over the feline duties."

"Don't fret, Gwen. Amber's no problem. I'll take care of your golden brat until I know Jenna is back."

"Thanks, Liz."

"Happy to do it. Hopefully, the drowning was an accident, and your hostess will soon be off the hook. Are you planning to do some snooping on your own?"

"No one besides Ben and the Nantucket detective knows, but I'm working behind the scenes. I'm officially sleuthing."

Liz laughed. "Why am I not surprised? All I can say is that Julie is lucky you're on the case. Maybe Tess will join you like she did before. Safety in numbers and all that. If someone besides Julie participated in that woman's drowning, you need to be careful."

"I will, Liz, and thanks again."

After disconnecting, Gwen tapped her messages icon, seeing that yesterday's texts to both Liz and Jenna displayed a red notification to try again. Would that happen to any text to the mainland? Would texts also fail on Nantucket?

Chapter Eighteen
… mid-afternoon, Sunday

As Gwen was about to dial Jenna's cell number, she heard footsteps on the staircase inside and leaned forward to glance through the French doors of Julie's sunporch.

Ben and Julie stepped off the bottom tread.

Gwen heard him say, "If I have any more questions, I'll let you know that I'm coming back."

Julie's expression none too happy, she practically stomped off toward the front room.

Ben glanced to his right and spotted Gwen, entered the sunporch, and settled next to her on the flowered sofa.

"How did it go with Julie?" Gwen whispered.

He lowered his voice. "She protested Ferguson's suspicion, but I'm not sure what to make of her. She showed me the portrait of her captain and asked if I believe in ghosts."

Gwen's eyebrows lifted. "And how did you answer?"

"Merely that I'm open-minded."

"Did Julie mention our failed séance at the party?"

"She did. I was surprised you hadn't told me."

Gwen felt she'd let him down, so said, "We've been concentrating on Sylvia's drowning."

"No need to get defensive, Gwen. I was only curious."

They sat in silence as the seconds ticked by.

Ben broke the awkwardness. "Julie invited me to join you tonight for her cousin's second séance."

"Did you accept?"

"No, no. I explained it could be a conflict of interest. I have to tell you, Gwen, I was tempted, but chasing ghosts isn't the reason I was brought over to Nantucket."

"Meaning you need to be watchful, or Ferguson won't give your findings any credibility."

"Exactly." He glanced at a clock between sunporch windows and rose to his feet. "I'd better get back to my interviews. I'll check in before I leave."

***

When Ben entered the living room, Julie turned from the front windows. "I'm sorry for my terseness in the studio. As an apology, I'm extending an invitation."

Ben reacted with the expected response. "To what?"

"Instead of eating by yourself in town, why don't you stay and join us for dinner?"

"That's thoughtful of you," Ben began, "but avoiding a conflict of interest also applies to sharing meals."

"I should have expected that," Julie said.

Ursula raised her head from a photo album. "Speaking of dinner, cousin, you and I need to shop for groceries."

"You're right," Julie said. "We'll leave as soon as Ben finishes his chats with you and Tess."

***

In the studio, Ben jotted Tess's memories of party night in his wire-bound book for comparison to the others.

After standing, she turned to him. "Ben, I know I'm biased, but I can't imagine Julie was responsible for Sylvia's fall."

"I can understand your loyalty to your college roommate. All I can do is follow the clues to the end. Would you please ask Ursula to join me up here?"

Tess nodded. Within a few minutes, Ursula appeared.

Ursula's interview revealed the same details about the events on Friday night, ending with, "I hope you don't think my cousin is responsible for that woman's death."

His response was similar to Tess's. Though he sympathized with their allegiance, he avoided jumping to conclusions without facts to back up Julie's innocence.

As he and Ursula reached the first-floor landing, Julie appeared. "I'm ready to go grocery shopping if you are."

At Ursula's nod, Ben said, "That's my cue to leave. I'll be in touch if I need to speak with any of you again."

Popping into the sunroom, Ben said to Gwen, "I've finished for the time being. Want to walk me out?"

Gwen rose from the couch. "Of course."

When they reached his loaner, Gwen touched his sleeve. "Are you sure you want to refuse Julie's dinner?"

"It's best this way. Call me tomorrow when you're sure of your privacy. We can also text during the day."

"That's true, Ben, but texts out here aren't dependable. My messages yesterday to both Liz and Jenna didn't go through. If my return text doesn't arrive right away, your message wasn't received."

"I'll keep that in mind." Half glancing back at Julie's house, he leaned down and kissed Gwen's cheek.

Chapter Nineteen

… late afternoon, Sunday

Waving until Ben's black loaner rounded the corner, Gwen suspected that eyes were watching through the cottage's front windows. But when she entered the foyer, she found Ursula and Julie donning light jackets. Did that mean they hadn't been watching her and Ben?

Tess appeared from the front room. "Do you want me and Gwen to help with the grocery shopping?"

"No need," Julie replied, gathering her blonde ponytail outside the collar of her coat. "You two make yourselves at home. Ursula and I should be back in an hour or so."

"Well, okay if you're sure," Tess said, "but I fully intend to contribute to the cost."

"That goes for me, too," Gwen added. "But I'm glad to have some time to explore the bluff walk and maybe the beach while you're gone."

Ursula held the front door open for her cousin to exit, then the two hopped into Julie's green Jeep.

Gwen and Tess stood on the veranda, watching the bright vehicle vanish. With the breeze off the waters of the northern Atlantic lowering the outdoor temperature, the sisters hugged themselves against the early November chill.

Tess said, "I feel weird that they left us here alone."

"I do, too," Gwen agreed, "but Julie's right. Four shoppers in a grocery store would be two too many. Besides, I have something I want us to do."

"You mean explore the bluff walk?"

"And those steps down to the beach. Let's go, Tess."

They headed inside and up to their suite to retrieve their jackets before exiting through the sliding glass door and strolling across Julie's shallow lawn.

Directly ahead of them, the wooden platform brooded in the bright sunshine. If only it could talk, Gwen thought.

She placed both feet squarely on the structure and looked down. Sensing Tess at her back, Gwen pointed at the bottom of the run. "I can't imagine Sylvia tumbling all that way. If those railings hadn't stopped her, the storm surge might have washed her out to sea."

"That would've been even more tragic," Tess said, "because no one would have ever known what happened to her. Are we allowed to go down these steps?"

Gwen linked arms with her sister. "With the crime scene tape gone, I don't see why not." The two of them descended, free hands grasping the handrails until they reached the lowest platform. "Ben showed me photos of Sylvia's body."

Too late, she realized Tess wasn't aware of Gwen's agreement with Ben to work behind the scenes.

But Tess didn't even blink. "I suspected you might be partnering with Ben again because he invited you to lunch. And after his interview with Julie, you two whispered in the sunporch. Not difficult to figure out."

"I never could keep any secrets from you, big sister. Let's walk along the beach. Crystal lives further north, and I overheard her tell another guest that she lets her kids play in the sand every afternoon. I'm hoping to bump into her rather than knock on her door."

"Which costume was Crystal?" Tess asked.

"I think the disco dancer with the white boots."

"Oh, yea. Didn't she leave the party early?"

"That's right. Good memory. She wanted to get home to her children and husband."

Clambering down the end steps, their shoes touched the hard-packed sand. For a long moment, they stared across the seemingly endless water. Gentle waves lapped against the shoreline. The repetitive motion and sound mesmerizing, Gwen understood the appeal of living close to the ocean.

As squawking seagulls winged overhead, Tess took a stance in front of Gwen, blocking the sun from her shorter sister's face. "What will you be doing behind the scenes?"

With no beach walkers nearby, Gwen didn't bother to lower her voice. "Ben asked me to chat with the party guests because I've already met them. They'll be more likely to share local gossip with me. If the medical examiner's report wasn't delayed, it might have revealed an underlying cause for Sylvia's fall, but for now Detective Ferguson is assuming there was foul play."

"And suspecting my poor Julie."

Gwen placed a comforting arm around Tess's shoulder. "All I can do is gather information and share it with Ben. But I need to conceal my undercover status from Julie… and Ursula, too. Do you think either of them has figured out that I'm partnering with Ben?"

Tess shook her head. "If they gave the two of you any thought, they probably assumed you're lovers."

A bit embarrassed by the potential assumption, Gwen pretended interest in a broken shell.

Taking the hint, Tess dropped the subject and looped her arm through Gwen's, guiding them both toward the shoreline.

"But listen, Gwen," Tess said, her voice brooking no argument. "I want to be with you when you visit those women. If Sylvia's death wasn't an accident, the real culprit won't appreciate your constant snooping."

"That's nearly word for word what Liz said to me when I called and told her what happened."

Tess continued her lecture. "What Liz can't do is have your back out here. We need to stay alert. How much time do we have for our walk before Julie and Ursula return?"

Gwen checked her cell phone. "I'd guess about a half hour. Let's continue along the beach." She gazed along the sand, a memory forming.

"Tess, do you remember on Saturday morning, when the detective and patrolman were on the beach one minute and walking toward us on the bluff path the next?"

"I do," Tess answered. "They must have climbed up using another access point. Based on how quickly they reappeared on top, a second set of steps can't be too far from here."

"Right. Let's try to find it for our return to Julie's so we can say we checked out the walk along the bluff."

When they rounded the next outcropping of the bluff, they spotted two adults plus children romping on the sand.

Tess pointed. "Do you think that's Crystal?"

Squinting to focus, Gwen answered, "Hard to say, but the young family is a clue. Let's say hello."

The sisters quickened their pace, shouting over the pounding of the surf, "Crystal?"

The young mother shaded her eyes. "Who are you?"

Gwen stepped closer. "From Julie's party. I'm Gwen Andrews, the ghost, and this is my sister Tess, the witch."

Laughing, Tess said, "She doesn't really mean that."

Pausing for only a second, Crystal giggled, "Of course. If I hadn't left early, I might have recognized you both... sorry."

When the suntanned man reached for the squirming baby, Crystal introduced him as her husband.

Shifting the child into his other arm, he said, "I'll leave you to talk," and cajoled the twins to race ahead of him.

Crystal turned back to the sisters. "I heard you joined Wyatt's search for his missing wife."

Wondering which guest had updated Crystal, Gwen jumped at the opening. "Did you also hear that her body was found at the bottom steps in front of Julie's house?"

121

Crystal nodded. "I'm the one who found her."

Placing a gentle hand on the young woman's shoulder, Gwen said, "That must have been quite upsetting. Were your children and husband with you?"

"No, and I'm glad they weren't."

Tess moved to Crystal's other side. "Are you aware the police consider Julie a person of interest?"

Her eyes widened. "That's not what I expected you to add. I only met Julie recently, but she seems like such a nice lady. Any idea why the police suspect her?"

Gwen explained the nutmeg connection, plus Sylvia's accusation of an affair between her husband Wyatt and Julie.

Digging her toes into the sand, Crystal glanced sideways at Tess. "Do you think your old roommate should be blamed?"

Tess shrugged. "I hate to think so, but I haven't spent any quality time with her since our days of sharing a dorm room."

Crystal squinted at the sun. "If Julie didn't push the woman, do you think someone else did?"

Gwen replied, "That's the question that needs to be answered. Tess and I don't know anyone on Nantucket, so we have no idea if someone held enough resentment against Sylvia to follow through with such a tragic act."

Providing this opening for Crystal to share local gossip, Gwen stopped talking.

"I've bumped into Sylvia several times on the bluff walk," Crystal offered. "She was always tipsy. Have the police considered she might have stumbled on her own?"

"That's one possibility," Gwen agreed.

Crystal stared down at her buried toes. "Her husband could have faked his search to cover his involvement."

Studying the young mother, Gwen said, "Your mind works in an interesting way."

With a subtle shake of her head, Crystal half-laughed. "I watch a lot of murder mysteries when the kids are taking a nap." Then her face lit up. "Wait a minute. Molly said that Nikki went downstairs to ask Sylvia not to report our party noise to the association. That would mean Julie wasn't the last person to see Sylvia alive that night."

Gwen was already aware that she'd been so distracted by the captain's portrait, she'd paid little attention to Nikki's return. Knitting her eyebrows in concentration, Gwen turned to Crystal, "I don't recall what Nikki said about Sylvia when she rejoined us in the studio. Tess, do you remember?"

"Not really. She was dripping wet from the rain and Julie handed her a dry towel."

At that moment, the baby screamed, "Mommy!"

Her husband approached, the twins racing ahead of him.

"Sorry," Crystal apologized. "I need to get back to my family. If Sylvia's drowning wasn't an accident, I hope the police arrest someone other than Julie. Goodbye."

Crystal hurried along the beach, nearly knocked down by her twins as they wrapped their arms around her legs.

Gwen and Tess waved to the family, then continued their search for the next exit from the beach. Less than fifty feet further on, they spied a rise of squared boulders leading upward at a slant. Climbing, they reached the dirt path at the top and turned left toward Julie's house.

As Gwen walked beside Tess, she said, "Nikki is the next guest we should visit."

Chapter Twenty
… late afternoon, Sunday

Up in the guest suite, Gwen retrieved Ben's journal gift from the zippered compartment of her luggage and settled at the small round table near the window.

When Tess emerged from their shared bathroom, Gwen waved toward the other chair "Have a seat."

Tess indicated the journal. "That's pretty."

"A gift from Ben to keep track of my sleuthing activities."

"Very thoughtful."

When Tess made no further comment, Gwen said, "I need to write down our conversation with Crystal."

As the sisters agreed about Crystal's comments, Gwen jotted down the details.

That task completed, Gwen drew a line. "Now let's add our opinions about her as a suspect."

"You first," Tess said.

"For one," Gwen began. "Crystal left before Sylvia crashed Julie's party, so she wouldn't have been aware of the encounter with Julie about her husband's presence."

Tess straightened. "And we know that Crystal walked north to her home. According to Wyatt, Sylvia entered the Bluff Walk from their house in the southern direction."

"Right," Gwen agreed. "Even if they'd encountered each other that early, the timing's off." She recorded these first bits of analysis.

Tess added, "Crystal mentioned that she'd seen the tipsy Sylvia during walks but didn't say they'd ever spoken and didn't offer any gossip, either positive or negative."

"Crystal doesn't strike me as a person who might have tangled with Sylvia on that platform."

"I agree, Gwen. Will Ben object to me tagging along?"

Shaking her head as she closed the journal, Gwen said, "I can't be sure. He'll probably appreciate that you volunteered to guard my back. But both Ben and Detective Ferguson were adamant that my C.I. participation remains confidential. When I speak with Ben, I'll find out what he thinks we should do."

Nodding in agreement, Tess lifted her nose like a hunting dog on point. "Do you smell that?"

Gwen sniffed the air. "I didn't hear Julie and Ursula return from their shopping. They must think we're still out walking. Smells like they've started supper."

Grasping Tess's shirt sleeve, Gwen stopped her sister from rushing downstairs. "Hold on a minute."

"Why? I'm suddenly starving."

"Don't mention our beach chat with Crystal."

"Why not?"

"Because Julie can't suspect that I'm part of Ben's investigation. If she thinks I'm snooping around as Liz puts it, she'll be too careful about what she says around me. After all,

126

it's much too early for Ben to determine if she's innocent as she claims."

"Oh, I hope you're half-joking, Gwen. My heart would break if Julie was the person to cause Sylvia's death."

"Well, until facts and evidence prove the case either way, all of our visits with Julie's friends need to have a logical reason for taking place."

Tess's face fell. "Unfortunately, you're right. Let's go."

Hurrying downstairs, the sisters poked their heads into the kitchen. "Need any help?"

Julie jerked away from the stove. "Oh, I didn't realize you'd come back from exploring. Did you enjoy the bluff walk?"

"We did," Tess answered. "Also strolled along the sand for a while."

"Did you dip your toes in the water?"

"Not on your life. That water must be frigid." Tess peeked over Julie's shoulder. "Whatever you're cooking smells delicious. What can we do?"

"Nothing. Dinner's ready. You two go sit."

In the dining room, Tess moved to the sideboard and called out, "Want me to pour this wine?"

Across the foyer, Julie appeared in the kitchen's wide archway. "Sure. Ursula and I bought that cranberry apple variety at a local vineyard."

Tess half-filled the four wine glasses.

Not to be outdone, Gwen sliced the warm loaf of cranberry pecan bread and placed the basket on the table.

Ursula and Julie carried in salads of torn spinach, cranberries, and feta beneath a raspberry vinaigrette, instructing the sisters to take their seats.

Standing, Julie lifted her glass. "Bon appétit."

Gwen and Tess both raved about the salad. Next, Ursula placed individual plates of bay scallops sauteed in garlic butter over angel hair, lemon wedges, green beans, and butternut squash at each placemat.

After finishing her meal, Gwen put down her fork. "That was delicious. I'm stuffed."

"Thank you," Julie said, adding, "I didn't want you to miss out on the seasonal scallops."

Ursula glanced around the table. "Dessert, anyone?"

"I'm too full," Gwen answered.

"So am I," Tess echoed. "But let us clear the table."

Ursula raised her near-empty wine glass. "Thank you."

After the plates were carried to the kitchen, Julie pulled Gwen aside. "When you walked Ben out to his car earlier, did he mention our discussion in my studio?"

Unsure of what Julie really wanted to know, Gwen chose the safest topic. "Do you mean showing him your captain's portrait and asking if he believed in ghosts?"

"Yes," Julie confirmed. "Ben turned down my invitation to join our séance this evening."

Relieved that Julie didn't suspect Ben had shared the interview details, Gwen relaxed. "He's always careful to avoid a conflict of interest during an investigation."

As if she hadn't heard Gwen's response, Julie barreled ahead. "Could you ask him to drive back and join us? Having a man within our circle might encourage my captain to appear."

Ursula came up beside them. "During all my séances, I've never noticed that a man sitting around my table encouraged a male spirit to appear."

Gwen added, "And I don't feel comfortable putting pressure on Ben to disregard his professional ethics."

Slumping, Julie said, "Oh, all right. I'll drop it."

Back at the sink, Ursula hand washed the four wine glasses and placed them in an upper cabinet.

Julie slanted a glance at Gwen. "Thanks for suggesting Ben come to Nantucket to investigate Sylvia's drowning. I didn't intentionally grate nutmeg into her eggnog to make her dizzy. There's no way I could have predicted that she'd stumble from that platform. I wasn't even aware she'd be interrupting our party to find her husband."

Though guessing, Gwen said, "I can't imagine that the nutmeg is enough to hold you responsible for Sylvia's tumble. Ben will uncover what really happened that night."

"Even if it was an accident?"

Gwen repeated the question as a statement. "Even if it was an accident."

Tess approached. "You wouldn't know this, Julie, but Gwen here helped solve suspicious death cases that stumped the local police back in Harbor Falls."

Julie stared at Gwen. "You did?"

Surprised at Tess's unplanned revelation, Gwen glared at her sister and squirmed under Julie's blue-eyed scrutiny.

"It's true, Gwen," Tess confirmed, then turned back to Julie. "My sister has become quite an amateur sleuth. The first time, she proved herself innocent, then did the same for wrongly accused friends and family."

Julie reached for Gwen's hand. "Would I be taking advantage if I asked you to do the same for me?"

"I don't know, Julie. Back home, I was familiar with the people in my community. That's not the case out here."

Gwen was reaching to protect her C.I. status.

"But you've already met my party guests, so they're not total strangers. I hope none of them are responsible for Sylvia's death, but they might know a local who held a grudge against Wyatt's wife."

"That's true." Gwen pretended to mull over Julie's request, which exactly matched her own plan. "I'll do what I can, but I make no promises. If I bump into any of your friends while I'm on the island, I can at least encourage a conversation. And if I hear anything of interest, I'll tell Ben so he can follow up."

Julie threw her arms around Gwen's neck. "You've eased my worry. Thanks."

Gwen admitted to herself that Tess's surprise revelation and Julie's reaction had just made her C.I. role much easier.

But was Gwen courting her own conflict of interest by playing both sides? Vowing to ask Ben when she called him later, she pushed aside her concern, seeing no reason to delay.

"How well do you know your party guests?"

Julie's forehead wrinkled. "I met them on my walks, shopping, at the post office. I only know where some of them live or work… if they do… and a little personal info."

Nodding her understanding, Gwen continued. "If I'm going to accidentally bump into them, those details would come in handy. Could you create a list, no matter how insignificant the details may seem?"

"Of course. Give me a sec to grab a sheet of paper."

Sitting around the dining room table, Gwen watched as Julie jotted down what little she knew about her party guests. Was Tess's college roommate hiding anything? Gwen would compare Julie's new list to the one she'd supplied to Detective Ferguson to check if anything didn't match.

Ursula strolled over from the kitchen, wiping her hands on a dishtowel. She sat in the adjacent chair and placed her hand on Julie's wrist. "Excuse me, cousin. I won't interrupt you long, but I have no commitments back home. I can stay a bit longer if you want."

Julie reached over and hugged Ursula. "I'd love your support, so yes, please stay."

Turning her gaze to Gwen, Julie said, "I can't expect you to be my personal sleuth without inviting you to remain in my guest suite. You should stay, too, Tess, if you can."

The task of booking other lodging no longer necessary, Gwen looked at Tess. When her sister nodded, Gwen answered, "That's very generous of you, Julie. We'd love to stay. More opportunity to enjoy your cottage at the beach and the rest of the island as well."

"Then it's settled," Julie stated with a half-smile. "All three of you will remain my guests for an unknown number of days until Detective Ferguson drops his accusation. Ursula, what time do you want us to gather for tonight's séance?"

Tess cleared her throat. "Sorry, but count me out. Friday night was enough for a non-believer like me."

Ursula was quick to respond. "No need to apologize. Until you meet your first ghost, you have every right to question whether or not they exist."

Leaning back in her chair, Tess half smiled. "Thanks. You have a kind heart."

"Cousin," Julie said, "should we refer to you as Ursula or Madama Eudora?"

A coy smile spread across Ursula's lips. "I'll answer to either. How about we meet in your studio at nine o'clock."

Tess stood up. "I'm heading up to our suite to read." Her footsteps soon echoed on the staircase treads.

Julie tapped Gwen's arm. "Do you have anything to take care of between now and our séance?"

"As a matter of fact," Gwen answered, "I can use the time to make a few phone calls I've been putting off."

Julie picked up her pen and repositioned the list. "I've got a few more details to add. I'll bring this to you when we meet later for the séance."

Chapter Twenty-One

… mid-evening, Sunday

When Gwen opened the door of their guest suite, she spotted Tess sitting at the small table near the window.

In the distance, the moon skittered across the quiet waters of the Atlantic Ocean.

So engrossed in her book, Tess didn't seem to notice either the door open or someone enter.

Gwen called, "Tess?"

Lifting her head from the page, Tess adopted the deer in the head-lights expression. "I didn't hear you come in."

"The story you're reading must be a page-turner."

"Sure is. I'll pass it to you when I'm finished. Why are you back here so soon?"

"Ursula's séance doesn't begin until nine. for another half hour. I'm going to call Ben."

But when she lifted her cell phone, she noticed a blue dot at the email icon. Gwen opened the waiting reply from Jenna, which read:

> *'Sorry I haven't been in touch. The cell service in Vermont is spotty at best. I totally understand that you're staying on Nantucket to help Tess's college roommate out of a jam. Good luck with that.*

My classmates and I had a fantastic time. Hiked Stratton Mountain and visited an old country store. I convinced them to visit the Will Moses' gallery on Grandma Moses Road just over the Vermont line in New York! He paints a more detailed version of his grandmother's style. I remembered you assembling a jigsaw puzzle with a similar motif, so I bought you one of Will's. You're welcome!

The four of us will be driving toward Harbor Falls in another hour. I should be back in time to feed your feisty feline a late supper.

Until you return from Nantucket, I'll keep the home fires burning, so to speak.

Please stay in touch! Love, Jenna

Touched by Jenna's thoughtfulness, Gwen sent a warm reply without any details about Sylvia's drowning.

Next she left a voice message telling Liz that Jenna was on her way home, so continued Amber duty was unnecessary.

Sitting across from Tess at the small table, Gwen said, "Ready for our chat with Ben?"

Nodding, Tess tucked a bookmark in her story.

When Ben answered on the second ring, Gwen said, "Hi, Ben. Tess is with me. You're on speaker phone."

"Hello, Tess."

"Hi, Ben. I may cause a problem with my intention, but I insist on partnering with Gwen when she goes snooping."

Gwen interrupted. "Sorry, Ben. As much as I tried to conceal it, my sister is too perceptive."

Ben said nothing for a long moment, then, "Well, Tess, thanks for watching your sister's back but this adds a bit of a complication to our arrangement. I'll have to inform Ferguson, and he will either have Tess sign a confidential informant agreement or he'll want you both off the case. We'll deal with that tomorrow."

Relieved that Ben was not upset with them, Gwen gave him a moment to absorb their news.

His voice boomed through the speaker. "What happened after I declined Julie & Ursula's dinner?"

Tess proceeded to describe their scallop dinner in detail.

Then Gwen shared Julie's pressure to change Ben's mind about returning for the séance.

"Thanks for repeating my conflict of interest. She seems determined to be friends with me, which I just can't allow."

Tapping Tess on the arm, Gwen pointed at the speaker. "Tell Ben what you pulled at dinner."

Tess explained that she revealed Gwen's past sleuthing successes. Julie took the bait and asked for Gwen's help to refocus Detective Ferguson's suspicion onto someone else.

"Kudos, Tess," Ben said. "Now Julie won't question your visits with her friends. Gwen, did you play coy?"

"I had to! Didn't want Julie to suspect I'm already collaborating with you. Julie invited me and Tess to remain as guests until her precarious situation is resolved."

"Be careful. She thinks you're searching for other suspects to remove her from Ferguson's scrutiny, but you're also scrutinizing Julie herself. Don't share what you and Tess uncover unless Julie asks."

Ben's yawn echoed through the speaker.. "Anything else?"

"Yes," Gwen answered. "Should I be concerned about my own conflict of interest because I'm staying in Julie's home during our investigation?"

"You're officially unofficial," he replied, "so you don't need to be concerned."

"By the way, "Gwen continued, "did you know that the woman who found Sylvia's body was a party guest?"

"No. How did you make that connection?"

"Crystal told us herself."

"How did that happen?"

"Tess and I bumped into her during our beach walk this afternoon. We mentioned Sylvia's drowning, and Crystal shocked us with her involvement."

Opening the journal, Gwen located Crystal's notes and condensed the young mother's words for Ben's benefit. "We hoped she'd suggest someone who resented Sylvia, but she didn't offer any local gossip."

Ben asked, "How about Crystal herself?"

Tess leaned toward the speaker. "I didn't sense any animosity toward Sylvia. Plus, Friday night's timing was off."

Gwen said, "And I doubt Crystal would risk separation from her family. We don't consider her a suspect."

"If no incriminating facts about that young mother come to light, that's one down," Ben murmured.

"She did remind me and Tess that Nikki had gone downstairs to ask Sylvia not to report the party noise. We can't remember what Nikki said when she returned, and Detective Ferguson didn't have a statement from her, so we're planning to visit her at the yoga center tomorrow."

"If this Nikki did speak with Sylvia," Ben began, "then Julie wasn't the last person to see Wyatt's wife alive."

He stopped talking to let this assumption sink in.

Having nothing else to discuss with Ben, Gwen said, "Which restaurant did you choose for your dinner?"

"Didn't need one. Maeve served me a delicious chicken casserole, and then I helped her wash the dishes."

A foolish tickle of jealousy brushing her, Gwen teased, "Cozying up to the innkeeper?"

Ben chuckled. "Well, it never hurts to stay on the good side of the woman who cooks your meals. Was the séance successful? Did Julie meet her captain?"

"We're not trying again until nine o'clock."

"Well, good luck with both the séance and your interview tomorrow. Be mindful that anyone you speak with could be the culprit."

"If there was a culprit," Gwen reminded him. "Tess and I are hoping Sylvia's death was an accident."

"I know. I know. Let's see where the rest of our interviews lead us."

Tess made a comment. "Maybe your visit with Ferguson's wife will fill in a few blanks."

"Remains to be seen. I'll let you know how Ferguson wants to handle Tess's involvement. Let's talk tomorrow night. If there's nothing else, I'll let you two enjoy the rest of your evening. Good luck with the séance."

Ben ended the call and was gone.

Since it was closing in on nine, Tess returned to her mystery, and Gwen headed up to the third-floor studio.

***

Disconnecting, Ben exhaled a lungful of air.

With Tess included in the speaker conversation, he said nothing to Gwen about her recent coolness. When she told him she'd suggested that Jake Ferguson request his assistance on Nantucket, Ben had been heartened about their future because Gwen was his perfect mate.

But would the two of them ever move beyond mystery-solving partners and good friends to become a real couple?

Chapter Twenty-Two

… late evening, Sunday

Entering the studio, Gwen found Julie repositioning three chairs around the table beneath Captain Tiffin's portrait.

Julie glanced up. "Is Tess settled in for the night?"

"She is. Did you remember to bring your list?"

Reaching into her pocket, Julie withdrew a sheet of paper and held it out.

On a quick scan, Gwen saw the same names, home addresses, and phone numbers Julie had provided to Detective Ferguson. The additions now were workplace… if any… marital status, how they'd met, and miscellaneous details. After skimming the words, Gwen folded the page and tucked it in her own pocket. "Thanks for putting this together, Julie."

Lifting her shoulders, Julie said, "I never realized how little I know about my new friends. I hope it's helpful."

"I'm sure it will be."

"I'd just like to add that I can't imagine any of them pushing Sylvia down those steps. I'm hoping they can point you at someone else."

Gwen placed her hand on Julie's shoulder. "We won't know what happened until the investigation ends. There's still the possibility that her death was an accident."

During Gwen's sleuthing in Harbor Falls, the guilty party had become nervous and tried to put a stop to her questioning. Each time, the culprit had been the one Gwen least suspected.

Who would it be in the case of Sylvia's drowning? Or would they discover that she fell without a push?

Julie spoke. "During your previous experiences of rescuing wrongly accused friends, have you ever…"

An alarm dinged on Julie's smart watch, cutting short her question. "I can't believe it's almost nine. I need to check if Ursula's up from her nap."

Rushing to the frosted door, Julie nearly collided with Ursula, transformed by the costume of Madame Eudora.

"Where are you going in such a hurry, Julie?"

Gwen was again amused that Ursula's voice had reverted to the sultry tone of the medium she'd met several years before in Harbor Falls.

Moving to the seat nearest the captain's portrait, the medium reached into her séance tote and placed a single candlestick in the center of the low table, then laid down the familiar herbal braids. She waved Julie and Gwen into the chairs, murmuring, "Let's begin."

Grasping first the sage, then the sweet grass, she performed both lighting ceremonies, repeating the chant to fend off negative spirits while inviting positive ones. Then she implored Captain Percy Tiffin to appear.

After three failed attempts, Madame Eudora said, "I'm sorry, cousin. Shall we keep trying?

Julie slumped in her chair. "I'm beginning to think the tales I've been told about him are simply far-fetched stories for kids at Halloween with no basis in fact."

Empathizing with Julie's disappointment, Gwen sat forward, focusing on Madame Eudora. "Should we try to connect with my Parker?"

"Excellent idea," the medium replied, "He was quite entertaining when he manifested during my séance at your dining room table. When did he last appear?"

Her back stiffening, Gwen stretched as she answered. "A few days ago. I'd driven to our gravesite to call him but was intercepted by the groundskeeper. When I got home, Parker manifested in my gardens."

Julie gasped. "How fascinating. Does Tess know?"

Shaking her head, Gwen said, "A few years ago, she sat in on Ursula's séance in my dining room but didn't see any of the spirits that appeared. That confirms my sister's stoic non-belief in the paranormal. I'm quite sure she'd doubt my sanity, Ursula, and maybe yours, too."

Gwen opted not to mention her own brush with death and Parker's ghostly promise to be waiting for her on the other side.

Ursula reached over. "Has your Parker appeared anywhere besides your property in Harbor Falls?"

"Not technically," Gwen answered. "Last winter, he manifested in my home, then floated beside me across the village green to the B&B. He searched for and spoke to their resident ghost."

Ursula paused for a moment. "But he's never appeared to you in any other location?"

At Gwen's negative shake of her head, Ursula continued. "Then let's call your Parker here to Nantucket and find out if he can join us."

Julie slid to the edge of her chair, her voice edgy with anticipation. "Maybe he'll agree to search for my captain like he did at the B&B."

Because the candles had not yet burned down, and the scent of the fragrant herbs lingered, Ursula joined hands with Julie and Gwen before calling Parker's name.

There was no response.

Gwen repeated Ursula's summons.

Again, no response.

Thinking her mounting anxiety might link them, Gwen upped the desperation in her voice.

Still nothing.

Then Julie begged Parker to drop in for a visit and try to find her captain's ghost.

After a repeated effort, the three women sat back in their chairs, disheartened by their failure to connect with either the captain or Parker.

In an attempt to lighten their disappointment, Gwen said, "It appears our ghosts haven't returned from their Halloween hauntings."

Ursula snickered, removed her turban, and shook out her long black hair.

Gwen snuffed out the candle, picking up the partially burned herbs. "Are these enough for your next séance?"

Inspecting the lengths, Ursula nodded and zipped each into plastic bags before tucking them into her tote.

As Gwen turned toward the frosted door, she said, "I'll see you both in the morning."

Descending one level to the second floor, Gwen continued down the hall toward the guest suite, mulling the possible reasons for Parker's no-show.

Had he lost his ability to sense Gwen's mood or hear her voice? Had the universe imposed a limit on the number of times Parker could appear on earth? She pursed her lips in frustration. There was no way to verify the possibilities until she returned to Harbor Falls and called Parker's name in their library home.

Determined not to further risk her link to Parker's spirit, Gwen debated whether to tell Ben about the failed attempt to bring Parker's ghost to Julie's studio. Again, she persuaded herself not to mention Parker to Ben. Nantucket during their investigation was not the time or place to explain Parker's promise, the reason for her coolness toward Ben. She'd wait until the two of them had returned to Harbor Falls.

Not wanting to disturb Tess, Gwen gently pushed in the door of their guest room, stifling a chuckle when she heard soft snoring from the second bed.

Chapter Twenty-Three

… early morning, Monday

The next day, as Ben sat down at the breakfast table, Maeve bustled through the swinging door, a pot of hot tea in one hand, a jar of honey in the other.

As her only guest, Ben chatted with her each time she served another breakfast food. First, fruit salad, followed by a bowl of porridge, then bangers and mash with toasted crumpets, sweet butter plus marmalade.

When she returned to remove his dirty dishes, Ben patted his belly. "Delicious, Maeve. You're spoiling me."

She blushed. "Thank you, Mr. Snowcrest. If my guests are pleased, they may return for another stay."

"I just may do that," Ben half-promised, though he filed the thought in the back of his mind.

In his room, he reviewed the contents of the case file, the interviews in the notebook. After jotting questions to ask Ferguson's wife, he located the second post-it note and dialed Mrs. Ferguson's number.

She answered on the third ring and invited Ben to their home for a cup of coffee.

Fifteen minutes later, he entered the Madaket Beach region on the western shore of Nantucket. Locating the property on a quiet side street, he parked in front of a modest house. As he walked toward the front door, he admired the leaf-free lawn and flower boxes of colorful autumn blooms.

Pressing the doorbell, Ben waited. On the other side of the plank slab, he heard a vacuum running, so he pressed a second time. Running feet replaced the hum of the machine, and the door flew open.

Ben stood eye to eye with a tall woman, her brown hair a bit disheveled, but a smile on her heart-shaped face.

"Detective Snowcrest?"

He nodded and handed her a business card.

After reading the information on the card, she waved him in, pointing to the blue-themed room on her left. "Make yourself comfortable in the parlor. I'll bring our coffee."

By the time Ben had settled into an overstuffed chair in the corner, Mrs. Ferguson carried in a tray loaded with two coffee mugs, a sugar bowl, and a carton of light cream. Though Ben's stomach still stretched from Maeve's bountiful breakfast, he picked up one of the mugs and drank the coffee black. Not his favorite cinnamon hazelnut that Gwen brewed, but a different flavor that he found equally enjoyable.

"I'll bet Jake didn't tell you my first name, did he?" She lowered herself to the sofa. "It's Adelaide, but Jake insists there are too many syllables, so he calls me Addie. To anyone else, he simply refers to me as 'his wife' or 'the wife.'" She shook her head. "Despite my efforts, he's a case of old dog, new tricks. Now tell me what you want to ask about Sylvia Pierce."

Although she didn't sound as distraught about Sylvia's death as Ferguson had implied, Ben appreciated Addie's direct approach. From his briefcase, he pulled out his list of questions and a pencil.

She answered each with little emotion. How long they'd known each other. The last time Addie had spoken to Sylvia. The moment Ben asked about Sylvia's accusation of an affair between Wyatt and Julie, the front doorbell chimed.

"Excuse me, detective. I'm not expecting anyone." Addie hurried to the door.

Her voice lowered to an urgent whisper. The visitor responded with equal urgency. When the door closed behind them, their voices became muffled.

As Ben scribbled a note in the margin about the odd interruption, the front door opened and closed as a vehicle engine sped away and faded.

Addie returned to the parlor, pushing her disheveled hair away from her flushed face. Reaching for her mug, she gulped a sip. "Now where were we?"

Not expecting her to reveal who she'd chased away, Ben answered, "I was about to ask if Sylvia told you her suspicions of Wyatt's affair with Julie Robinson."

Addie flicked her hand in dismissal. "Same thing Sylvia says about every female Wyatt meets during his carpentry projects. After a while, I stopped listening."

Recalling that party guest Evie had said the same thing, Ben made a note of confirmation. "Do you know of anyone who wanted Sylvia out of Wyatt's life?"

With wide eyes, Addie stared. "Jake and I are... were... casual friends of the Pierces. We've gone out to dinner, and played a card game or two, but I was hardly privy to her enemies, if she had any."

"One last question. Did Sylvia ever indicate she wanted to end her life?"

"Not directly to me. Wyatt mentioned a while back that she was seeing a medical professional, but whether that was a psychiatrist or some other specialist, he didn't specify. You'd better ask him."

Addie placed Ben's half-empty mug on the tray, then added her own plus the sugar bowl and carton of cream, signaling the interview was over. "I'll see you out."

Ben had gained enough answers for the moment, so thanked her for her time, then listened to the lock click after she closed the door behind him.

***

Pulling into an empty parking lot around the corner, Ben flipped through the case file until he found Wyatt's address in Sconset, a few numbers south of Julie's cottage.

His investigator's mind swirling around Addie's change of attitude after she chased away the unknown person who knocked on her door, Ben decided to pay Wyatt an unannounced visit rather than warn Sylvia's husband of an impending second interview.

Chapter Twenty-Four

… early morning, Monday

Gwen settled on a chair in their suite, pondering the most efficient strategy for sleuthing. On the next blank page in her journal, she sketched a rough silhouette of Nantucket Island.

Pulling up an online map, she located each address from Julie's embellished guest list, jotting their initials coded 'H' for home or 'W' for work on her island outline.

When Tess emerged from the guest suite bathroom, she peeked over Gwen's shoulder. "What are you doing?"

"Noting where each guest lives or works."

"That should come in handy," Tess said. "Are we still planning to drop in on Nikki today?"

"Yes, but we need wheels."

"Maybe Julie will let us borrow her jeep."

"Maybe," Gwen repeated, holding up one finger as a reminder. "Don't forget we can't mention yesterday's beach chat with Crystal or that she's the one who found Sylvia's body at the bottom of Julie's steps."

"You're right," Tess agreed. "Julie hadn't asked us to investigate on her behalf until dinner last night."

As they began to descend the staircase, Julie placed one foot on the bottom riser and looked up.

"Oh, there you are. I was just coming up to tell the two of you that breakfast is ready."

Gwen initiated their plan. "Tess and I were discussing Nikki's activity on Friday night."

"What activity was that?" Julie asked as she waved them into the dining room where Ursula was placing a steaming stack of French toast.

Tess replied, "When you returned to the studio after your private chat with Sylvia, Nikki hurried downstairs to request that she not to report our party noise."

"Yes, I remember that now."

"Do you recall what Nikki said when she returned?"

Julie's eyebrows scrunched, wrinkling her forehead. "Not really. I was showing the rest of you the portrait of my captain before handing her a towel for her wet hair."

Gwen took over. "Neither of us can remember what Nikki said either."

"No surprise. It wasn't that important at the time. Why is her comment important now?"

"If Nikki spoke to Sylvia…" Gwen began.

Julie's eyes lit up. "…that means I wasn't the last person to speak to Sylvia!"

"Exactly."

"But what if Nikki didn't talk to Sylvia?"

Gwen made a wild guess. "It's possible that other people were watching the storm. They may have noticed Sylvia on your platform and whether she was with anyone."

"But if there was anyone else out in that storm, won't the police have spoken to those people?"

"Not necessarily. Tess and I want to visit the yoga studio and have a chat with Nikki. How's the bus service into town?"

"Not very quick because of all the stops," Julie said. "I'd let you borrow my Jeep, but I have a dentist appointment this morning. After today, you can use it anytime. I'd suggest an Uber driver. With the summer crowds mostly gone, they're hurting for passengers."

Julie rummaged in a drawer and held out a list of names and phone numbers. "I'll see the two of you later."

***

When a car horn beeped out front, the sisters hurried down the front walk, waiting for the driver to confirm Gwen's name before sliding into the back seat.

"Where to?" the grey-bearded man asked.

After Gwen provided the address in town, the driver stepped on the gas, soon pulling in front of the yoga studio.

He handed Gwen his card. "Call when you're ready to go somewhere else."

She paid the fare and tucked his card in her tote bag.

Entering the studio, they spotted Nikki demonstrating yoga poses to women of all shapes and sizes.

When she came out of a downward dog position, she met Gwen's gaze, and mouthed *'Five minutes.'*

Nodding that she understood, Gwen plucked a free street map from a stack on the studio's windowsill.

Tess snatched a yoga brochure and sat in a plastic chair at the front windows. "I should join my local yoga studio."

"Good idea," Gwen agreed, settling in the adjacent chair. "In Harbor Falls, a new exercise center opened next door to Liz's bookshop. Maybe I'll do the same."

Within minutes, the class disbanded. The women rolled up their mats and tucked them into oversized tote bags.

Nikki rushed over to Gwen and Tess. "Here to sign up, ladies? I'm running a special two for one offer."

Gwen quickly realized that Nikki... like Crystal... did not recognize either of them, so she offered a clue. "Looks like we just missed your session. We were intrigued with the idea after you mentioned your studio at Julie's party."

Tittering, Nikki said, "Of course. You're the sisters. Which of you was her college roommate?"

Tess raised her hand. "I'm Tess, and this is Gwen."

"Now I remember you." Nikki repositioned a chair to form a conversation triangle and sat down. "Her costume party was such fun."

Aware Nikki hadn't answered Detective Ferguson's knock on Saturday morning, Gwen saw no reason to delay. "Did you hear about Sylvia Pierce's drowning?"

Nikki's eyes widened. "One of my earlier class members mentioned a drowning over in Sconset. I didn't know it was the woman who barged into Julie's party."

Gwen continued. "The police spoke to us after Crystal found the body during her morning beach walk."

Nikki shook her head. "That must have been so upsetting for the poor girl."

"When the police questioned the four of us," Tess added, "the detective asked Julie for a list of her party guests so they could take statements."

"No one asked me for a statement," Nikki protested. "But then, I scheduled an early class on Saturdays, so maybe I wasn't home when they stopped by."

"To make a disturbing situation even worse," Gwen continued, "the detective returned and informed Julie that she's a person of interest in Sylvia's death."

Nikki shifted in her chair. "Why does he think Julie had anything to do with that woman's drowning?"

"Partially because of the nutmeg connection," Tess said. "He claims it may have made Sylvia dizzy."

Gwen added, "But mostly because Sylvia accused Julie of having an affair with her husband."

Huffing, Nikki said, "Well, that's just ranting from an insecure wife with a drinking problem. Didn't Evie say that Sylvia accused *her* of an affair with Wyatt while he was updating her kitchen?"

Tess straightened. "Do you think Evie was involved with him during her project?"

"Hard to say. Evie does tend to flirt, but Wyatt's too old for her. I can't imagine she'd be interested in him."

Gwen sat forward. "Can I ask you another question?"

"Sure." Nikki glanced over to the door.

"After Julie joined us in her studio, she mentioned that Sylvia threatened to report our party noise."

"That's right," Nikki agreed.

Tess took up the thread. "Then you went downstairs to ask her not to. Did you actually speak with Sylvia?"

Nikki's forehead wrinkled. "She wasn't on the patio. I dodged the raindrops to the edge of the lawn and looked both ways on the bluff walk. But I never spoke to her."

"Did you notice anyone else?"

Nikki's eyes flew open. "Yes! Further up the path, some kooks were dancing in the puddles. I thought they were nuts to risk a lightning strike. When the rain circled back again, they scattered, and I rushed back to Julie's patio. That's why my hair was dripping wet."

The yoga center door opened, and three laughing women entered, dressed in patterned workout gear.

When they called a greeting, Nikki waved before returning her attention to the sisters. "My next class is arriving, so I've got to go. But I'll say one last thing."

"What's that?" Gwen asked.

"You should chat with Molly. I left the party behind her, and she walked in the other direction on the bluff path. If she bumped into anyone, she might have known them. She knows a lot of people who live on the island."

Stepping to a display of business cards on the windowsill, Nikki extended one. "Here's Molly's card, her shop isn't far. Do you want to join my next class? It's hot power yoga."

"Thanks, but that sounds way above our level," Gwen answered. "Maybe we'll come back for a beginner class." Gwen accepted Molly's card and grasped the street map.

"The schedule is on my Facebook page," Nikki called as she hurried toward her students.

Gwen and Tess exited, barely avoiding two more women in leggings rushing inside through the door.

Halfway up the block, the sisters sat on an empty bench, and Tess waved to indicate the nearly empty street. "There aren't many shoppers downtown today."

"Maybe the retail stores are closed on Mondays, plus the summer crowd is gone." Gwen pulled out her journal. "We need to record Nikki's input."

Tess leaned closer. "Nikki caught on that we're trying to get Julie off the hook. Do you think she'll tell the other party guests what we're doing?"

As Gwen wrote down the yoga instructor's comments, she answered, "Let's hope not. That might scare the others from sharing their observations. We need to be crafty when we chat with them as concerned friends of Julie."

Tess asked, "May I play devil's advocate?"

Gwen waved her hand. "Be my guest."

"What if Nikki made up everything she just said to us? What if she spotted Sylvia on the platform, got into a shoving match, and Sylvia tumbled down the steps? Extra time outside in the rainstorm would explain why Nikki's hair was soaking wet when she returned to Julie's studio."

Gwen stared at her sister. "Interesting theory. You're really sinking into sleuthing mode."

"Only because I desperately want to prove Julie innocent."

"Nikki's only one potential suspect. We need to continue our subtle behind-the-scenes interviews."

"Do you think Molly could be another suspect?"

"Why do you jump to that assumption?"

"Well, when Sylvia showed up drunk, Molly was downright mean, as if she was already mad at the woman."

Gwen paused before reacting. "At this point, you and I are just spouting theories." She flipped the business card over. "Here's Molly's shop address. Let's visit her now."

Unfolding the street map, Gwen traced the streets with her finger in a crooked line. "A few lefts and rights will bring us to her shop's door."

Rising from the bench, they strolled along the sidewalk. None of the stores they passed appeared to be open, so neither sister had to battle the urge to shop.

But Gwen couldn't resist pausing at a flower box filled with autumn blooms. "Too bad these will wilt with the first frost."

With a touch of her hand on Gwen's sleeve, Tess pointed at the street sign ahead of them where they needed to turn.

Before they reached the intersection, a gentleman exited an old-time drugstore and the aroma of toasting bread wafted to Gwen's nose. "Are you hungry, Tess?"

"Now I am. Molly can wait a bit. Let's eat."

The gentleman grinned and held the door open.

Chapter Twenty-Five

… early afternoon, Monday

Their bellies filled with BLTs and clam chowder, Gwen and Tess paid their checks and hopped down from their stools at the old-fashioned counter.

Out the door to the sidewalk, they headed for the next intersection a half-block ahead when a green Jeep whizzed through the cross street.

Gwen asked, "Do you suppose that's Julie?"

"Most likely," Tess said. "What are the chances of two lime green Jeeps on Nantucket?"

Gwen shrugged. "No idea. Let's chat about Molly. I'll go first. I was standing at the patio door when everyone headed home so can vouch for Nikki's comment that Molly left first."

"Did you notice which way she turned?"

"No, it was too dark, and I wasn't paying any attention."

"Then if Sylvia was still roaming around out there, it's possible Molly bumped into her."

"But what's her motive for pushing Sylvia down the steps?"

Tess paused in thought. "If she wants Wyatt for herself, she might eliminate his alcoholic wife. Just a guess."

"We're still speculating," Gwen said as she pulled out Julie's handwritten list of guest details. "Let's see. Molly never married. We need a sense of her attitude toward Sylvia and Wyatt, whether positive or negative."

As they zig-zagged up one street and down the next, Gwen threw her arm across Tess's upper chest to halt her progress. Pointing her chin at the building ahead, Gwen asked, "Isn't that where Hester volunteers?"

"The Whaling Museum? I don't think that's right."

Gwen paused. "I read somewhere that the museum is run by the Nantucket Historical Association. Let's pop in and ask if Hester's on duty today. I don't remember her last name so give me a sec to check the guest list."

A minute later, they entered the colonial building and approached the reception desk.

"Hello. Is Hester Lawrence on duty today?" Gwen began.

The woman smiled. "Do you have an appointment at the research library?"

"No," Tess answered. "This is a personal visit."

Picking up the desk phone, the woman dialed, engaged in a brief conversation, then replaced the receiver. "I'm sorry, but Hester's not scheduled today. She'll be here first thing in the morning if you want to come back."

Thanking the receptionist, the sisters headed out.

"Well," Gwen said, "looks like we're coming back to town tomorrow."

"I wouldn't mind touring the museum," Tess added.

After turning one last left, they spotted a sign hovering above the sidewalk with *Island Textiles* carved in fancy lettering. Several women chattered as they bustled out the door, their arms struggling with oversized shopping bags.

Gwen entered ahead of Tess, causing the bell above the door to jangle wildly. They were instantly surrounded by the pleasant scent of new textiles displayed on shelves, racks, and various hangers.

As Gwen fingered a particular piece on the first table, Molly made her way over from the back of the shop.

"Good afternoon, ladies. Can I help you find anything in particular?"

When they both turned, recognition lit up Molly's face. "Didn't I meet you both at Julie's party?"

Gwen flattered Molly by saying, "You have a much better memory for faces than I do."

"Thanks, but wait..." Molly's eyebrows knitted in concentration before her eyes widened. "Julie's college roommate Tess, and her sister Gwen?"

"Wow. Not only faces but names as well. Very impressive," Gwen said. "Tess and I admired the throw Julie bought here, so we thought we'd check out your other designs and colors."

"Glad I brought business cards to hand out at the party," Molly bragged. "And you're in luck, ladies. A new batch of items was delivered by my favorite local artisan just this morning. Give me a sec and I'll bring them out."

Tess leaned toward Gwen. "How will we bring up Sylvia?"

"I'll think of something," Gwen whispered.

A minute later, Molly was barely visible above the stack of textiles she carried. After laying each piece carefully across the nearest table, she said, "Here you go." The shop's phone rang, and Molly turned. "Let me know if any of these will blend with your décor back home."

Spying a throw that echoed the neutral soft greys and soothing beiges of her living room, Gwen debated whether to buy it. She hadn't planned on a genuine shopping excursion and would have to carry the piece until they re-connected with their Uber driver.

As Gwen fingered the softness and texture of the material, Molly returned and noticed her choice.

"That one's a beauty. I doubt it will stay in my shop for very long."

"Oh, go ahead, sis," Tess encouraged. "Treat yourself."

Gwen again touched the supple fibers, her decision made. "You talked me into it. Ring me up."

At the counter, Gwen extended her credit card. "Did you hear about Sylvia Pierce's drowning?"

Molly tapped the register keys. "Yes, I did. I won't be a hypocrite and say I'll miss that unpleasant woman. It's a wonder Wyatt didn't divorce her years ago. The man was a saint to put up with her drinking for so long."

Before Gwen could encourage more comments, the bell above the shop door tinkled. Molly held out the oversized shopping bag, bid the sisters good day, and rushed over to greet the newly arrived customers.

Chapter Twenty-Six

… mid-afternoon, Monday

From Madaket on the southwest coast of the island, Ben maneuvered the two-lane roads, then the cobblestoned streets of Nantucket town, continuing out the other side toward Sconset on the east coast.

Parking in front of Wyatt's Cape-style house a few lots shy of Julie's cottage, Ben sat quietly to collect his thoughts. When he strolled past a work van in the driveway, he heard the engine click and placed his hand on the hood.

Warm.

Though he avoided making unfounded assumptions, Ben wondered if Wyatt had been Addie Ferguson's visitor. Then again, the man could have been driving his work truck for lots of other reasons, resulting in the same warm engine.

At the front door, Ben grasped the heavy knocker and let it fall with a loud bang. After fifteen seconds, he lifted and dropped it a second time. Placing his ear against the door, he heard no footsteps or shouts of *'I'm coming.'*

On a whim, Ben decided to take advantage of his proximity to Julie's. He'd inspect the platform and its steps to the beach. The day before, he'd only viewed both from her third-floor studio window.

As he cut through Wyatt's side yard, a door slammed around the back. Ben halted, then crept to the corner for a peek.

Ahead of him, a man hustled across the lawn toward the bluff, cell phone plastered against his ear.

Though Ben had yet to meet Sylvia's husband, he assumed that the salt-and-pepper-haired guy was indeed Wyatt Pierce.

Curiosity and instincts merging, Ben followed the man along the dirt path at a discreet distance. Though muffled, the words drifted back to Ben's finely tuned ears:

'We need to talk. I'm walking toward your place.'

He paused while the other person spoke.

'I don't care if your houseguest is upstairs. Meet me outside your sunporch where she can't see us.'

Three houses up, the man rushed across Julie's lawn.

Because the guy faced in the opposite direction, Ben kept moving along the path until he reached the hedgerow beyond Julie's property. With no idea if the neighbor next door was paying any attention, Ben crouched and slipped along the thick bushes, stopping when he came even with Julie's sunroom.

Peering through the crooked branches of the windblown hedge, Ben caught sight of Julie as she emerged around the front corner of her cottage, shoving her arms into a jacket against the chilly ocean breeze.

When she reached the man, she stared up into his face. "Why are you here, Wyatt? I have houseguests."

"A friend of mine at the police station told me Ferguson is trying to blame you for Sylvia's drowning."

"You think I don't know that?" Julie snapped.

"Of course *you* know that, but *I* just found out. Is Ferguson right to suspect you?"

Julie backed up. "How can you ask me such a thing?"

Wyatt shrugged. "For years, Sylvia and I have been… had been… friends with the Fergusons. Jake doesn't usually jump to conclusions. Why would he suspect you?"

"Because Sylvia accused me of having an affair with you?"

Wyatt released a bitter laugh. "Sylvia's accused me of sleeping with clients for years. Are you aware that Ferguson brought a detective over from the mainland to investigate my wife's drowning?"

"Yes. His name is Ben Snowcrest."

Wyatt's head jerked. "How do you know that?"

"Because the sister of my college roommate, who came over for my party and is staying with me, suggested him."

"I don't get it. Why did she do that?"

"Because Ferguson mentioned he's shorthanded, and Gwen said Ben might be able to assist with the case."

"I'm well aware that the department is short-staffed. That's why dispatch couldn't send anyone to help me search for Sylvia on Friday night. Did you know that Snowcrest interviewed Ferguson's wife Addie earlier today?"

"I'm not privy to his process," Julie snapped. "Why does that particular interview bother you?"

Wyatt ran his hand through his wavy hair. "There's no need for Snowcrest to draw Addie into this."

162

"Is Addie the one you're having an affair with?"

"Now you're sounding as looney as Sylvia."

When Julie touched his sleeve, he shook her off, half-turned and pointed across her lawn toward the platform.

Ben ducked even lower, but it didn't appear Wyatt had glanced toward the hedge.

"I wish we'd found Sylvia on Friday night before she fell down those steps," Julie told him. "She was drunk, you know."

"I'm well aware she'd been drinking,"

Ben noted a sadness in Wyatt's voice.

Julie said. "I regret offering her that cup of eggnog with extra nutmeg. That's Ferguson's other reason for suspecting my involvement in her death."

When Wyatt said nothing, Julie turned to leave. "I've got to go before my houseguest comes looking for me."

Wyatt reached over to stop her. "Wait a minute. During our search, you warned your guests not to risk slipping on those steps to the beach. Do you realize one of them might have spotted Sylvia and called for help?"

Her nostrils flaring, Julie pushed his shoulder. "Are you the one who told Ferguson about my cautionary warning?"

Wyatt stared at her. "Just part of my statement. You never answered my question. Is Ferguson right to suspect you were involved in my wife's drowning?"

Julie stiffened. "I could ask you the same question. Goodbye." She spun on her heel and headed back the way she'd come.

Wyatt didn't move until she disappeared around the corner, then he shot across her lawn without so much as a glance in Ben's direction.

Not budging from his hiding place, Ben absorbed their conversation. Abandoning his plan to inspect Julie's platform and steps, he snuck quietly along the hedgerow until he reached the dirt path.

With Wyatt ahead of him, Ben maintained a safe distance until the man ducked into his yard. Ben waited until the door banged shut before slinking along the side of the house for the return to his unmarked sedan parked out front.

Opening the driver's door, Ben slammed it closed to fake that he'd just arrived. Ambling again to Wyatt's front door, he hefted the weighty knocker and let it drop, this time hearing Wyatt's lumbering footsteps inside.

When the door jerked open, Ben extended his card. "My name is Benjamin Snowcrest. Are you Wyatt Pierce?"

As Ben's name registered, Wyatt half-closed the door, "Yes, I'm Wyatt Pierce."

"First of all," Ben began, "please accept my sincere condolences for the grim death of your wife."

Wyatt's face revealed his emotional struggle. "Thank you Mister…" Wyatt glanced down at the card. "…Snowcrest. Why have you come to see me?"

"Your Detective Ferguson brought me over from the mainland to investigate your wife's drowning."

"So, you're not an official Nantucket police officer?"

"That's correct."

"And why did Detective Ferguson think he needed you?"

"Because he and his wife have been friends with you and your wife for years. He needed an independent investigator to avoid a conflict of interest. As a retired detective with years of experience, I'm available to consult with any county that requests my assistance."

Wyatt's head swayed. "As far as I'm concerned, my wife simply lost her footing during Friday night's storm and stumbled. A tragic accident. A deeper probe by the police is totally unnecessary."

Cloaking himself in his most sympathetic expression, Ben adopted the interview techniques he'd honed over the years. "I understand your resistance to the idea that someone wanted to harm Sylvia. If you'll allow me to ask a few questions, I'll leave you to the rest of your day."

Wyatt swung the door wide and waved Ben inside. "Let's not stand out here for the neighbors to gawk at."

When Wyatt's stomach growled, he added, "I didn't eat breakfast and now it's past lunchtime. I'm going to make myself a grilled cheese sandwich. Want me to make you one as well? We can eat while we talk."

***

Gazing around Wyatt's kitchen, Ben noticed two half-empty bottles, one a vodka, the other a nutmeg liqueur. Had Mrs. Pierce mixed her own cocktail on Friday night? If yes, Julie grating nutmeg into Sylvia's eggnog would have been irrelevant to the woman's possible dizziness. The medical examiner finding nutmeg in Sylvia's bloodstream might not point the finger at Julie after all.

As Ben waited for his sandwich from the panini grill, he spoke to Wyatt's back. "I've been told that your wife was a bit tipsy when she arrived at Julie Robinson's home. How well do you know Ms. Robinson?"

Wyatt's back stiffened before he whirled around to face Ben. "I knew Julie as well as any client."

"Are you aware that your wife accused Ms. Robinson of having an affair with you?"

Wyatt forced a laugh. "I'm not surprised. My wife thought I seduced every female customer."

Ben guffawed. "Insecure women can be a challenge. Must have made your homelife a bit tense."

Plating the sandwiches, Wyatt handed one to Ben. "You've got that right. Beer?"

"Not while I'm working."

"It's non-alcoholic, if that makes a difference."

"Thanks, but water will be fine."

Handing Ben a bottle of water, Wyatt sat opposite and popped the top from his bottle of beer. "It's nice to have the taste of beer without alcohol. Sylvia never liked the taste of beer – only the hard stuff."

Between bites, Ben alternated case questions with personal condolences. Wyatt's answers all sounded honest and his occasional emotional hesitation sincere. Sensing Wyatt was

166

getting antsy, Ben wiped his mouth with a paper towel and slid his chair back. "I'll be going now. Thanks for the sandwich."

"Not at all," Wyatt responded. "Be sure to let me know what you discover about Sylvia's drowning."

Standing on the front step, Ben turned back. "One last question, Wyatt. *Are* you and Julie Robinson having an affair?"

Instead of answering, Wyatt scowled and slammed the door in Ben's face.

Because the husband was always the primary suspect, and despite Detective Ferguson's claim that Wyatt shouldn't be suspected, Ben needed to check the man's AA alibi.

After leaving Wyatt's home, Ben pulled off to the side of Baxter Road and googled the local Al-Anon group. When he called the number, the outgoing message advised that the office would reopen at 10am the next day. Though disappointed, Ben moved confirmation of Wyatt's attendance at the Friday night meeting to the next day in his phone calendar.

Chapter Twenty-Seven

... mid-afternoon, Monday

Scooting out the door of Molly's shop ahead of Tess, Gwen nodded toward another bench and headed that way. She placed her bulky *Island Textiles* bag beside her, then retrieved the tapestry journal. "Let's record Molly's comments."

After writing the conversation as verbatim as their memories would allow, Gwen turned to Tess. "What do you think of Molly as a potential suspect?"

Tess hesitated. "No surprise to hear her negative opinion of Sylvia after verbally attacking the woman at Julie's party. If I had to guess, I'd say Molly always harbored a wish for Sylvia to be out of Wyatt's life."

"Do you think she has a crush on him?"

"That's one explanation, but it's a big jump. She seemed determined to cut our conversation short when new customers walked in. But I have no idea if she'd resort to violence."

Gwen noted Molly's possible motive, one of the three requirements to suspect a crime has been committed.

"What's your take on her ability?" Tess asked.

"Well," Gwen said slowly, "after watching her heft that armload of heavy textiles, she's certainly strong enough to push Sylvia down those steps. How about opportunity?"

Tess thought before speaking. "Well, Molly left the party by the bluff walk, so she could have bumped into Sylvia, if the woman was still wandering about outside."

Gwen recorded this third requirement and closed the journal. "I'll let Ben decide if he wants to interview her. How about we visit Evie on our way back to Julie's cottage?"

Tess pushed herself to her feet. "The one that Sylvia accused of an affair with Wyatt?"

"That's the one. She was Little Red Riding Hood and mentioned working at the mid-island grocery store."

"I remember her," Tess said. "If she's not working this afternoon, she'll become another delayed chat."

"We won't know until we try." Gwen dialed their Uber driver, and in less than five minutes he arrived.

**

Politely turning down the Uber driver's suggestion to leave her Island Textiles shopping bag in his back seat until he picked them up again, Gwen carried her purchase into the grocery store and placed it in a shopping cart.

Red-headed Evie wasn't ringing out a customer or bagging groceries, so the sisters approached the idle female cashier at the nearest register.

"Is Evie Henderson working today?" Gwen asked.

The gangly blonde pointed toward the back of the store. "Try the break room about halfway along the rear wall."

Gwen and Tess moved up the closest aisle, eyeing the Halloween candy, its prices slashed.

"Let's buy some for Julie's living room bowl," Tess suggested, touching a few bags as she passed.

Gwen groaned, her penchant as a dedicated chocoholic surfacing. "Maybe on our way out."

Entering the break room, they glanced around.

No Evie.

A female employee slumping at a table lifted her head. "Can I help you find something?"

"Yes. A cashier up front said Evie's on her break."

"She was here a second ago," the girl offered. "You might check the ladies' room one door down."

Sure enough, they nearly collided with the height-challenged Evie as she exited the bathroom.

"Oh, I'm sorry, ladies. I should know better than to rush out without looking."

"Not a problem, Evie," Tess began. "Do you remember me and my sister Gwen from Julie's Halloween party?"

Evie studied both their faces, finally shaking her head. "Sorry, I don't. What were your costumes?"

Gwen mentioned her ghost and Tess's witch, then remembered another detail. "We changed out of our costumes to join Wyatt Pierce's search party for his wife."

Evie again stared at their faces. "Of course. I'm terrible at remembering faces unless I spend one-on-one time with a person. Why did you two track me down?"

Gwen didn't want Evie to hurry back to her register before providing at least one pertinent detail. Evie could have bumped into Sylvia after the party. But did this petite young woman have the strength to push someone off that platform?

Realizing she'd hesitated, Gwen hurried to say, "We're picking up a few things for Julie and remembered your quip about mis-bagging groceries. Thought we'd say hello while we're in your store."

Evie laughed. "So, I'm an afterthought? Just kidding." She eyed the Island Textiles bag in the cart. "You bought something at Molly's shop. Can I see?"

"Sure," Gwen said, thankful for the excuse to worm their way into a useful conversation.

"That's gorgeous. I'm sure you've picked out the perfect spot back home."

Describing her converted library, Gwen mentioned her leather sofa then refolded the throw and re-bagged it.

"Sounds like a delightful place to call home. Has Julie recovered from her party and the séance?"

Grateful for another opening, Gwen looked at Tess, then back at Evie. "From the party, yes, but on Saturday afternoon, Detective Ferguson nearly arrested her for Sylvia Pierce's drowning."

"What?" Evie shouted, then covered her mouth, too late to silence her outrage. "He questioned me the next morning about their confrontation. I hope I didn't say anything that that made Julie look guilty."

Reaching out to calm Evie, Gwen said, "He spoke to all the party guests after he chatted with the four of us…"

"…except for Nikki," Tess inserted.

Evie frowned, waving the sisters toward a door. "Let's go outside where we can talk." She pulled out her cell phone and set a timer. "I've got another ten minutes."

After they settled on opposite sides of a picnic bench set atop a concrete slab, Evie lowered her voice. "Isn't Nikki the one who went downstairs to convince Sylvia not to report our party noise to the neighborhood association?"

"That's right. On Saturday afternoon, Julie pointed out to Detective Ferguson that he hadn't interviewed Nikki."

"Well," Evie continued, "Nikki will surely confirm chatting with Sylvia after Julie returned. Any idea if the detective has caught up with her?"

"Not that we've been told. This morning, we stopped by Nikki's yoga studio to check the timing of her classes and mentioned Julie's predicament. Nikki said she never did find Sylvia that night."

"That's strange," Evie countered. "Seemed like Nikki was gone quite a while. But it was *a dark and stormy night,*' as they say, so who knows?"

Gwen kept the conversation light but also focused until Evie's cell phone timer dinged, and she hopped to her feet, her eyes again ping-ponging from one sister to the other.

"Sorry, I have to go back to work. Thanks for letting me know what's been happening."

Holding the door for them, Evie rushed toward the cash registers at the front and was soon out of hearing range.

Gwen turned to Tess. "Evie didn't point the finger at any of the other guests."

"She might have if we'd had more time with her," Tess said. "But right now, we need to buy a few things to back-up our reason for being here. Let's wheel this cart around and pick up whatever strikes us."

As they checked out at Evie's station, the red head whispered, "I'm glad you two are staying to support Julie. I hope she's cleared soon."

***

Five minutes later, the sisters' Uber driver screeched to the curb and hopped out to store their grocery sacks plus Gwen's shopping bag in his trunk. Soon after that, he dropped them at Julie's front walkway. "I'll wait to hear from you ladies when you need another ride." And he sped down the driveway.

As Julie stored the groceries, Gwen noticed she was unusually quiet and glanced over at Ursula, who was leaning against the archway.

Ursula crooked her finger for Gwen and Tess to follow her through the living room, then outside to the patio.

"Julie's been sullen for the past hour. I heard her talking to someone outside a while ago, but I couldn't see who from the upstairs window."

Gwen paused to think. "Maybe we should wait for her to share what's bothering her."

Ursula shrugged her shoulders. "If she doesn't snap out of her doldrums by supper, I'll ask her."

***

An hour later, cooking aromas lured Gwen and Tess to the kitchen to find Ursula busy at the stove.

"Can we help?" both sisters asked at once.

Ursula turned, her eyes expressing her surprise. "Oh, I thought you were Julie."

"Where is she?" Tess asked.

"Went for a walk. Said she needed to think. She's been gone for a while."

Behind them, Julie's voice called, "I'm back."

Holding a spatula aloft, Ursula studied Julie as she entered the kitchen. "You're limping. What happened?"

Julie pointed down at her foot. "Someone whizzed by on Baxter Road. I lost my balance and sprained my ankle."

"Let's have a look." Ursula guided her cousin to a dining room chair and removed her sneaker. "Your ankle is swelling. We should take you to the emergency room."

Julie waved off the concern. "No need. I hurt my ankle when I first moved here, so I know it's not broken." She winced as she rotated her foot in confirmation.

"At least let me prepare an icepack." Ursula rushed toward the kitchen freezer.

"I've got a boot upstairs," Julie called, "which is all any doctor would recommend."

"Where is it?" Tess asked.

"In the back of the master suite closet."

"Be right back." Tess rushed up the staircase.

Ursula returned, lifted Julie's lower leg to the adjacent chair and balanced the icepack atop her ankle.

Tess bounded down the staircase with the boot.

And Gwen continued to fuss.

"All right, all right," Julie objected. "I'll be fine, but I'm starving. What are you cooking for supper? Smells good."

***

After devouring green salad with sautéed chicken chunks, honey mustard dressing, and chopped pecans, Julie laid down her fork. "Delicious as usual, Ursula."

"Julie?" Gwen began, "did you notice if that was a car, a truck, or an SUV that knocked you off balance?"

Shaking her head, Julie replied, "I didn't look up as I was falling. Why do you ask?"

"With Sylvia's investigation underway," Gwen replied, "I have to wonder who drove so close to you."

"I appreciate your concern, Gwen, but it was getting dark. I'm guessing the driver didn't see me. Now, if you don't mind, I think I'm going to head up to my bed to rest."

Refusing assistance, Julie hobbled up the staircase.

When Gwen heard the master suite door close, she posed a question to Ursula and Tess. "Do either of you think the speeding car was suspicious?"

Ursula sighed. "I don't know what to make of it. You're the amateur sleuth, Gwen. What do you think?"

"Until we determine if Sylvia's drowning was an accident or something more sinister, I'm suspicious of anything that happens around here." Gwen caught herself before saying she'd mention the incident to Ben, because neither Ursula… nor Julie… was aware of their partnership.

After minimal conversation, Gwen said, "I could use a distraction. How about we play a card game I learned recently called 'Unlucky Sevens'?"

"May as well," Tess responded. "Hope it doesn't take much concentration though. I'm worried about Julie."

"We all are," Gwen confirmed, turning to Ursula. "Does Julie own a pair of dice and a deck of cards?"

"I'll check the games in the sideboard."

Gwen added, "We each need quarters and dimes."

After an hour of play, Gwen glanced at Tess's huge pile of coins. "I declare you the winner, Tess. It's been fun, but I'm heading upstairs to make some phone calls. See you in the morning."

As she climbed one step at a time, it occurred to Gwen that Julie hadn't asked about their chat with Nikki.

***

Waiting until Tess joined her, Gwen dialed Ben's cell.

"Good evening, Gwen. Is Tess with you tonight?"

"I'm here," Tess confirmed.

"Good. Did the two of you uncover anything today?"

"We did, but first you need to know what happened to Julie a few hours ago." Gwen explained the whizzing vehicle that caused Julie to lose her balance and twist her ankle.

"She didn't notice the type and color?" Ben asked.

"No. Julie said she was too busy avoiding a more serious run-in," Tess answered.

"Okay," Ben said, his exasperation evident. "I'll make a note in my file and mention it to Ferguson. There's no way to know if her near miss is related to our investigation. For now, do your best to make sure she doesn't go anywhere by herself."

Tess aimed her voice at the cell phone's speaker. "We'll suggest that to both Julie and Ursula."

Gwen opened her journal. "Are you ready to hear what Tess and I learned today?"

"Yep, go ahead."

As Ben listened, asking a question here and there to clarify a point, Gwen retold their chat with Nikki at the yoga studio. Skipping over lunch at the old-fashioned drug store, she moved to their conversation at Molly's textile shop. And lastly, Evie at the grocery store.

As Gwen progressed from one conversation to the next, she included her reaction plus Tess's to the words and attitude of each party guest.

Ben's pen scratching in his own notebook echoed through the cell phone's speaker.

"You sisters make quite the team," Ben said. "I've asked Patrolman Bryce to canvas Julie's neighbors, see if any of them installed security cameras. If there's footage of any storm watchers, he might recognize local faces that Nikki was too far away to identify. Should I interview this Molly Burns?"

"Wouldn't hurt," Gwen said. "How was your day, Ben?"

Ben shared his coffee chat with Addie Ferguson, her mystery visitor, his drive to Wyatt's house to find a warm truck hood, then following the man to Julie's sunporch and eavesdropping on their conversation. Then his interview with the man himself, concluding that their possible affair was still an unknown factor in the investigation.

"Well," Gwen began, "Wyatt's visit could explain why Julie was so withdrawn this afternoon and not paying attention to traffic during her walk."

"Makes sense," Ben said. "But doesn't prove anything."

Tess jumped in. "What did Detective Ferguson say about me tagging along with Gwen?"

"I haven't spoken to him about you yet. Just keep on doing what you're doing until I have his official input."

"Fine with me," Tess said.

Ben cleared his throat. "If there's nothing else, let's talk again tomorrow night. You're both to be commended for your excellent behind-the-scenes input. Sweet dreams."

Chapter Twenty-Eight

… mid-morning, Tuesday

The following morning, because Ben had no specific plans until his 10am drop-in at the Al-Anon office, he allowed himself to fall back asleep until the aromas of breakfast urged him from his guest house bed. He showered and dressed before heading down to Maeve's dining room.

"Maeve," he said when she appeared through the kitchen door carrying a plate of bacon, eggs, and toast, "am I still your only guest?"

She laughed, then said, "You are, Mr. Snowcrest. This is the usual lull between the summer visitors and the Thanksgiving/Christmas crowd. I prepared you a simple breakfast this morning."

"Simple is perfect," Ben said, chewing with gusto.

"You have the house all to yourself."

"I'll be out and about most of the day."

Maeve sat in the chair opposite Ben, resting her chin on one palm. "How's your investigation comin' along?"

Ben saw no harm in a non-specific update. "My interviews are far from over."

"Well, good luck," Maeve commented, pushing herself to her feet. "Will you be wantin' lunch or dinner?"

179

"Not lunch, but one of your dinners will taste fine this evening. Do you need to know when I'll be back?"

She waved off his offer, then must have changed her mind, because she said, "Why don't you call or text me when you know your timing and I'll place a Shepherd's pie in the oven."

Nodding his approval, Ben cleaned his plate just in time for his cell phone to buzz. He glanced at the caller ID, saying, "Sorry, Maeve, I've got to take this."

She waved him off. "You go about your day. I'll see you later for supper."

As Ben climbed the stairs, he tapped into the call and said, "Good morning, Detective Ferguson."

"The patrolmen use my title, but you and I can be less formal. Call me Jake."

"Then I'm Ben." Rather than second-guessing the reason for the call, he waited.

Jake filled the silence. "My wife Addie told me about your conversation with her yesterday, but she didn't think she provided any clues that were helpful. Where did you go when you left her?"

Ben didn't mention Addie's unrevealed visitor. No need to stir up marital problems without confirmation. Instead, he explained his arrival at Wyatt's house, then following the man to Julie's home, the details of their overheard conversation, plus his chat with Wyatt as they ate grilled cheese sandwiches.

"What's your impression, Ben? Was Wyatt having an affair with Julie?"

Ben hadn't made up his mind about the affair. Julie and Wyatt hadn't acted like lovers. In fact, they'd questioned each other about involvement in Sylvia's death.

To Jake, Ben said, "Hard to say."

"Then I'll reserve judgement," Jake commented. "Besides, an affair doesn't automatically translate to the lover harming the spouse."

Hmmm, was Jake referring to Julie or Addie?

Already, Ben sensed that the Nantucket detective was rethinking his suspicion of Julie... too little evidence to point a finger at any one person this early in the investigation.

Ben continued his review. "By the time I called the Al-Anon office yesterday, they had closed. That's my first stop this morning."

"Glad you're double-checking Wyatt's alibi. Not that I think he had anything to do with Sylvia's death, mind you," Jake insisted, "but if he was present at that Al-Anon meeting on Friday, his window of opportunity to push Sylvia down those steps is reduced."

Ben said, "I'm unconvinced that anyone else was with her on that platform. An accidental stumble is still on the table as far as I'm concerned."

"You're right, Ben. Plus we're still waiting for the final autopsy report."

"You should know that when I was at Wyatt's, I noticed an empty bottle of nutmeg liquor, along with a nearly empty bottle of vodka. That might complicate the M.E.'s findings about the amount of nutmeg in Mrs. Pierce's stomach. Did Patrolman Bryce tell you I asked him to canvas Julie's neighbors for security video?"

"Yes, he did. Great idea to identify the storm watchers gathered above the bluff. Bryce has made some progress. I'll have him contact you directly."

"Good. He's a smart young man, Jake. You should seriously consider moving him into your detective unit."

"Oh, I am. Has your Gwen Andrews been helpful?"

"Definitely. We plan to compare notes each evening. Nothing conclusive yet, but we're far from finished with our interviews. Mine official, hers behind-the-scenes."

"Well, just keep working the case."

"I will. But, before I get sidetracked, I need to mention that Gwen's sister Tess figured out that we're collaborating and wants to be involved. I wouldn't mind Tess watching her sister's back. Do you want her to also sign a C.I. agreement?"

"Best to have all our paperwork official. I need them both to stop by the station and ask for me. What's her proper name for the document?"

Ben spelled out 'Contessa Walker'. "Oh, one other thing you should know, Jake. There was an incident with Julie last night, but I don't know if it's connected to our case."

"What happened?"

"She was nearly sideswiped as she walked along Baxter Road at sunset. She lost her balance and jumped off the tarmac, spraining her ankle."

"Did she identify the vehicle?"

"No. It was getting dark, and she was trying to regain her balance. Maybe it was just a careless driver."

"Maybe," Jake echoed. "I'll make a note of it."

In the background, Ben heard voices.

"Sorry, Ben, I've got to go."

"I've got to get going myself. Do you want me to report every day?"

"Only if you discover anything that will resolve poor Sylvia's drowning one way or the other."

Disconnecting, Ben pondered the conversation. Was it possible that Wyatt's affair was with Jake's wife and not Julie? He wondered now if Addie had been out on the bluff Friday night while Jake was working. If she was detected on any of the security videos, he'd need to interview her again.

In his room at the boarding house, Ben called Gwen to ask that both sisters stop at the police station and ask for Detective Ferguson so Tess could sign her own C.I. form.

After a second review of the Al-Anon website, Ben drove to the address. As he parked his sedan, he noticed a man unlocking the front door. Ben hurried over, flashing his investigator's license.

"Good morning, sir. My name is Ben Snowcrest. I'm investigating a case on behalf of Detective Ferguson. Do you have time to answer a few questions?"

The man leaned close enough to read Ben's name on the license before straightening. "Depends on your questions."

The man... who had yet to introduce himself... held the door open for Ben to enter. "What do you want to know?"

"I'm looking into the drowning of Sylvia Pierce. Did her husband attend your Friday night meeting?"

"Simple enough. Let's check the sign-in sheet."

He walked to a filing cabinet and removed two documents, handing the thicker one to Ben. "This brochure explains how we assist the relatives of an addictive person. Wyatt is a sad case. No matter which of our techniques he tried, his wife couldn't seem to shake her need for liquor."

While Ben read the brochure, the man perused the sheet of paper. "Yep, here's Wyatt's signature on Friday night. And before you ask, I recognize his backhand scroll. The meeting broke up around nine."

Ben tucked the brochure into his briefcase. "That's helpful, sir. Any chance I can get a copy of that sign-in sheet for Detective Ferguson's file?"

The man grunted and walked to a printer on a nearby desk, slapped the paper on the platen, pushed the button, and handed the copy to Ben.

Thanking him, Ben extended a business card and headed out the door.

As he approached his police loaner, he spotted a cruiser parked in the adjacent spot, then Patrolman Bryce leaning against the front bumper.

The younger officer touched his cap. "Good morning, Detective Snowcrest. I spotted your loaner."

Chapter Twenty-Nine

… late morning, Tuesday

After Tess signed the C.I. document in front of Detective Ferguson, the sisters drove into town and parked Julie's bright green Jeep a half block from the Whaling Museum.

The same female receptionist smiled behind the counter. "Welcome back, ladies. When Hester arrived this morning, I mentioned the two of you. She asked me to let her know if you visited the museum again."

"That was very thoughtful of you," Gwen said, impressed by the woman's courtesy toward tourists.

"If you'll wait over there, I'll call her."

Within a minute, Hester swirled through a nearby door, her face lighting up when she spotted the sisters. "How nice of you to stop by. Tess and Gwen, right?"

"You remember us?" Tess asked.

Hester laughed. "I have a knack for remembering faces, names, and places. It's a blessing and a curse." She peeked around the sisters. "Did Julie come with you?"

"No, she didn't," Tess said.

"Oh, that's a shame. I'd like to show her something in our portrait gallery. Would the two of you like a tour?"

Tess surged forward. "Yes. Where do we buy tickets?"

Hester waved her off. "No need. Come this way."

Instead of turning into the museum proper, Hester led them back through the door she'd come through just a few minutes earlier. Playing tour guide, she chaperoned the sisters from one section of the museum to the next, all the while sharing Nantucket history.

When they entered the portrait gallery, Gwen moved quickly to a particular painting. "Is this Julie's captain?"

"You have an exceptionally good eye, Gwen. After Julie showed us her portrait of Captain Percy Tiffin, I thought he looked familiar. You're looking at an earlier rendition of him."

"Julie was so disappointed when he didn't appear during our séance," Gwen murmured.

"Apparently," Hester quipped, a smile tickling her lips, "ghosts are unreliable. Please ask her to stop by one day soon."

"We will," Tess promised.

Hester's levity disappeared. "How is Julie holding up after Sylvia Pierce's body was found so close to her cottage?"

Relieved she didn't have to devise a clever way to bring up the topic, Gwen answered, "Not very well."

"Why is that?" Hester asked. "I admit I didn't care for that Detective Ferguson asking me about their confrontation at the party, but my discomfort has faded."

"Julie's situation is more serious," Gwen began. "After he spoke to you and most of the party guests, he returned to Julie's cottage and accused her of grating extra nutmeg into Sylvia's eggnog to make her dizzy, so she'd fall down those steps."

"Well, that's ridiculous. That woman was fall-down drunk when she banged on Julie's patio door. Besides, how would Julie have known that Sylvia would stumble from that platform? I hope that detective had more than that."

"He did," Gwen confirmed. "Sylvia had accused Julie of an affair with her husband Wyatt Pierce several times."

"Did he arrest her based on those two pieces of flimsy evidence?" Hester asked.

"Fortunately, no. She pointed out that he hadn't obtained a statement from Nikki."

"Nikki," Hester murmured. "The young woman who offered to warn Sylvia not to report our party noise?"

Tess stepped in. "Yes, that's her."

Hester signaled them both to follow her, reversing their direction until they exited into the gift shop.

"It's time for my lunch break. Why don't the two of you join me at my favorite café around the corner and we can continue our talk?"

Chapter Thirty
… mid-day, Tuesday

Ben stepped around his unmarked sedan toward the young officer. "Didn't we agree not to be so formal?"

Logan Bryce pushed himself off the front bumper of his cruiser. "Force of habit, Ben. Sorry."

"No apology needed. Detective Ferguson said you've had some success with the security footage from Ms. Robinson's neighbors who live along the bluff?"

"Yes, that's why I stopped when I spotted your loaner. I thought you'd prefer an in-person report."

"Have the neighbors on the bluff cooperated?"

"Somewhat. Several homeowners didn't answer my knock. A few handed me the disks of their footage."

"Have you viewed the frames yet?"

"Only a quick scan."

"When can I have a look?" Ben asked.

"Any time. They're set up at the station."

"Let's go. I'll follow you."

At the station, they entered a second-floor office filled with A/V equipment. "What are we looking for, Ben?"

"The best would be Sylvia Pierce all alone on Ms. Robinson's platform."

Logan pulled up the footage and began to scroll. "And the next best?"

"Mrs. Pierce walking along the bluff path after she'd left Julie's cottage. We'll compare the time stamps to the period when Ms. Robinson was surrounded by her guests."

Logan nodded. "Providing her with an alibi, at least for that specific timeframe."

"Exactly." Ben kept one eye on the frames gliding past in slow motion until a person stumbled along the path. "Stop. That could be Sylvia Pierce. I've only seen the photographer's photos of her body on the beach steps. Can you print the best frame for me with the timestamp? I'm thinking this might be before she banged on Julie's patio door."

"Sure." Logan concentrated, scrolling to the clearest image. Then he rummaged through a pile of printouts on a nearby table and handed one to Ben. "This is her DMV license photo."

"Thanks." Comparing the two images, Ben said, "I'd say that's definitely Mrs. Pierce."

They continued to observe women and men moving along the path. When one lone man kept glancing over the bluff, Ben shouted, "Stop. That looks like Wyatt Pierce."

Again, Logan rifled through the documents, handing over the husband's license photo.

"I met Wyatt yesterday," Ben revealed, "but let's compare the faces to be sure." He held the DMV picture next to the monitor, saying, "Can you zoom closer?"

Nodding, Logan did.

Ben said, "Definitely Wyatt Pierce." He glanced at the timestamp. "He must have been on his way to enlist Julie in his search for Sylvia."

Ben flipped through his notebook until he came to Gwen's account of Wyatt's request. "He told Julie he'd been checking the pathway as he walked north. This video confirms his claim. Can you make a print of this frame?"

Again, Logan complied.

They reviewed the remaining footage, printing only the frames with faces clear enough for identification.

"If we can identify these other people, Logan, we can ask if they noticed Sylvia along the bluff walk on Friday night."

Logan handed Ben the final printout and leaned back in his chair. "Sorry, Ben, no images of Sylvia Pierce on Ms. Robinson's platform."

"Disappointing," Ben agreed, "but we haven't gotten our hands on all the available footage yet." Reaching into his case file, Ben held out Julie's list. "Can you print the DMV photos of these party guests plus Addie Ferguson?"

"No problem, but why the detective's wife?"

"Just a hunch. Don't mention it to him."

Though Logan appeared uncomfortable, he nodded. "How soon do you need these?"

"As quickly as you can get your hands on them."

A movement behind them startled both men and they swiveled their chairs to see Detective Ferguson leaning against the doorjamb, his arms folded.

"I heard you two were viewing security footage in here. Anything helpful?"

Ben got to his feet. "You heard right. Logan just printed frames of Sylvia, then Wyatt, with timestamps for comparison purposes. There were other men and women walking the bluff path on Friday night that we need to identify and interview."

"Any footage of Sylvia Pierce in a struggle with anyone?" Ferguson asked.

"Not from these three security cameras. Can I borrow Patrolman Bryce this afternoon?"

"Why?" the detective asked, his tone sullen.

Ben stared at Ferguson. Had he changed his mind about Logan's assistance? Needing to clarify, Ben said, "He retrieved the footage we just reviewed, and I could use his help to canvas other bluff residents to obtain their security recordings or share anything they might have seen during the storm."

Jake's bushy eyebrows lifted. "Are you solving the case or looking for an alibi to clear Julie Robinson?"

Confused by Jake's negative attitude, Ben defended his methods. "We'll uncover whatever evidence exists."

"All right, then," Jake snapped. "You and Patrolman Bryce head back to Sconset. Keep me updated." He turned on his heel and disappeared.

Trusting his own instincts that Ferguson's irritation could be attributed to other stressors in the police station, Ben turned to Logan. "Did you make digital copies of those three disks for the police files?"

"Not yet. Give me a sec." After each recording was saved to the hard drive, Logan handed the originals to Ben.

"You see about printing those extra DMV license photos. Then we'll return these disks to the owners and continue our canvasing down the line."

"We driving to Sconset separately or together?"

Ben paused. He needed a second interview with Julie. "I'll drive myself. Where can I meet you?"

"There's a sandy pull-off on the northern end of Baxter Road where the bluff walk ends."

"Fine... I'll meet you there." Ben slipped each disk into its own manila envelope and jotted the house number on each outside flap.

***

Half an hour later, Ben exited his loaner as Logan's cruiser pulled into the sandy area beside him.

"Sorry, Ben, took me longer than I thought to print those DMV photos. Here they are."

Tucking them into his briefcase, Ben said, "Thanks. Now let's hope that the homeowners who haven't left the island for the season are willing to share their security footage."

Ben followed Logan along Baxter Road until they turned onto a dirt-track leading toward the ocean. When they came to a security fence, the pathway turned right along the bluff.

Logan stopped and pointed to his left. "The bluff has been eroding for years. Some of the older houses had to be relocated before they slid down into the waters."

"Didn't know it was so risky to live on this stretch of beach," Ben commented, wondering how far down the bluff Julie's cottage was situated and how long before the land beneath her property collapsed.

The first three homes they approached seemed closed-up for the season, though the lights of their security cameras signaled activity. Unfortunately, Ben and Logan could not access the digital equipment inside those homes.

When Logan knocked at the fourth house, a dignified man opened the door, his smile wide.

"Back so soon with my security footage, officer?"

Logan extended a manila envelope marked with the house number. "Yes, sir. Thank you."

"Anything useful?"

"I'll let the detective answer that question."

Ben extended his business card as his introduction. "May we come in and ask you a few questions?"

"Sure, sure," the man replied, opening the door. "I'm a mystery buff, so helping you fellas would be a feather in my cap. My wife's off shopping, so she won't be back for another hour or so."

As they settled on the sofa, Ben said, "We could use some help identifying a few of the faces captured by your security camera on Friday night."

Agreeing to try, the mystery buff recognized Wyatt based on carpentry work completed a few years earlier but didn't identify any of the other faces from the DMV photos.

"Sorry, fellas. Have you checked with the guy further down the bluff?"

Logan turned his remaining two envelopes sideways. "Either of these numbers?"

"Nope." The mystery buff opened his cell phone's contact file and recited the name and house number. "I'll call him to let him know you're on your way. He's more likely to talk with you if he hears from me first."

Ben and Logan thanked the mystery buff for his help, waving goodbye as he closed the door behind them.

They knocked at the forewarned neighbor's front door and were invited inside. Sorting through the prints, he quickly identified one man who lived at the far southern end of the bluff walk. He also confirmed that he himself wasn't out in the storm the other night, so hadn't seen Sylvia Pierce or anyone else for that matter. Still, he handed over the SD card from his security camera. "Good luck, officers."

Moving along the bluff path, Ben paused before Julie's cottage. "I need a second interview with Ms. Robinson. I don't know how long I'll be."

"Should I wait for you?"

Ben shook his head. "No. Before you drive this new SD card back to the station, return those other two original cards to their owners. Then talk with the resident at the southern end of the bluff walk. I'll meet you in your A/V office first thing tomorrow morning."

"Got it," Logan said. "What time?"

Ben considered the question. "Eight o'clock. See you in the morning."

As Logan continued south on the dirt path, Ben strolled across Julie's lawn to her patio and glanced up to see a security camera. No light blinked to indicate it was operational. He tapped on her glass slider.

Inside, Julie hobbled over, her expression revealing surprise to see him. She opened the door. "Hello, Ben. Do you have any good news for me?"

"Not yet." He pointed up toward the camera. "Tell me about your security set-up."

"Oh, that old thing. It's been here since I bought the cottage. One of these days, I'll hire an electrician to either repair it or replace the entire system. Why do you ask?"

His shoulders drooped. "If your camera had been working on Friday night, the footage would have probably shown Sylvia on your platform..."

Her face falling, Julie finished, "...and revealed the person who was with her."

"Unless Sylvia was by herself," Ben suggested. "Either way, Ferguson would have no option but to drop his suspicion of your involvement in her tumble down those steps."

Julie waved Ben inside, hobbled to the sofa, and placed her booted foot atop the coffee table.

Though Gwen had told him about Julie's sprained ankle, Ben pretended he didn't know and pointed at the boot. "What happened here?"

She described her evening walk when a car on Baxter Road passed too close and she jumped to the roadside.

Ben listened intently until she finished. "Any idea who nearly sideswiped you?"

"Like I told Ursula, Gwen, and Tess, it was getting dark, and I was trying to catch my balance. I can't tell you if it was a car or an SUV or even the color."

Ben sat in an adjacent chair and considered the incident. Had the near miss been merely a driver not noticing a person walking along the side of the road? If a warning, for what reason? Julie was already a person of interest in Sylvia's death.

If someone else had pushed Sylvia down those steps, they'd be more than happy to let Julie take the blame.

Ben thought back to her conversation with Wyatt the previous afternoon. Neither had hinted at an affair. Or guilt.

If Sylvia had been right to suspect Wyatt of fooling around, maybe the affair hadn't been with Julie at all. The possibility still irked Ben that Ferguson's wife could be Wyatt's lover. But Wyatt's warm engine yesterday morning was no proof that he'd been Addie's unknown visitor.

But if Addie *had* been Wyatt's lover, would she have wanted to eliminate Julie's competition for his affections? Had she been the one to sideswipe Julie?

Without evidence, playing the what if game was getting Ben nowhere. He forced himself back to Julie's clear blue eyes. "I'm curious why Wyatt asked your help to search for his wife. Tell me about your relationship."

Chapter Thirty-One
… mid-afternoon, Tuesday

After discussing Julie's legal situation with Hester over a late lunch of lobster bisque, Gwen and Tess walked the historian back to the Whaling Museum.

"Thanks so much for the museum tour," Tess said.

"And for showing us the portrait of Julie's captain as a much younger man," Gwen added. "We'll encourage her to visit you soon."

"Please do," Hester urged. "Seeing that portrait may provide her with a much-needed distraction."

As the sisters headed toward the jeep, they passed an empty bench and sat down… their favored and necessary routine.

Gwen plucked the journal from her tote bag.

Tess said, "Hester didn't contribute any new information."

"No, she didn't," Gwen agreed. "She was sympathetic about Julie's status as a person of interest but didn't point her finger at any party guests or share any gossip. Plus, she's not the first guest who claims never crossing paths with Sylvia until the party."

From the back of her journal, Gwen unfolded her rough map of Nantucket dotted with initials and codes. "Let's see if we can fit in another party guest before we return to Julie's."

"Before we do that," Tess interrupted, "I'd like to review the comments we've collected so far."

Gwen started with the beginning journal pages, condensing the remarks of each guest.

1. Crystal Young... *suggested speaking with Nikki about her follow-up conversation with Sylvia.*
2. Nikki Quinn... *mentioned Molly bumping into people on the bluff path after the party.*
3. Molly Burns... *not fond of Sylvia, conversation interrupted by arriving customers. Suggested Ben speak with her.*
4. Evie Henderson... *interested, but no contribution.*
5. Hester Lawrence... *sympathetic, no gossip.*

Tess held out her hand. "Can I see the guest list?"

Retrieving it, Gwen placed it in her sister's palm.

"These are the few we haven't seen yet. Tinker Bell Jasmin, '20's flapper Rose Griffin, and black jumpsuit Sandy Owens."

"I didn't chat with any of them during the party."

"Neither did I, but, then again, we devoted a good chunk of our evening to Wyatt's search." Tess stifled a yawn.

"Ready for a nap, sis?" Gwen teased.

"Seems so," Tess answered, her expression sheepish. She shook herself. "Five down, three to go. Which one should we visit this afternoon?"

As Tess watched, Gwen's forefinger traveled along the marked-up map, reciting the initials and names until she paused at the third one. "Jasmine works at a farm stand that's sort-of on our way back to Julie's cottage."

"Sounds good to me." Tess stifled another yawn.

***

Before exiting the Jeep, Gwen looked over at her sister. "You sure you're up for this?"

Tess said, "I'm a bit tired, but I'll be fine as soon as I walk around. In addition to finding Jasmin, let's also buy fresh vegetables for Julie."

"Good idea," Gwen agreed, "but let me call her first so we don't overbuy."

Moments later, Julie said into Gwen's ear, "That's our favorite market. I'm handing the phone to Ursula."

Jotting Ursula's preferences on an errant piece of scrap paper, Gwen stared at the huge barn with extensions on both ends. "This place is much bigger than a farm stand."

Once inside, they were quickly surrounded by vegetables, fruits, and baked goods. Tess said, "That's an understatement."

Rather than ask someone where to find Jasmine Nash, they strolled from one booth to the next, pausing to buy Ursula's veggies. It didn't take long to fill Tess's handled sack with broccoli, cauliflower, carrots, fennel, and celery.

Gwen's second canvas sack brimmed with apples, pears, and cranberries.

When they came to a fudge counter, Gwen recognized Jasmine even without her Tinker Bell costume. "Jasmine? Do you remember us from Julie's party?"

When Tess halted next to Gwen, Jasmine grinned. "I recognize you both. If you're here for my excellent fudge, I recommend Rocky Road. It's the perfect combination of sweet and salty. Would you like a taste?"

A devoted chocoholic, Gwen was not about to turn down the offer. But knowing that Detective Ferguson interviewed Jasmine the next day, Gwen was surprised the girl hadn't mentioned Sylvia's drowning.

Gwen reached for the sample and said, "Wasn't it awful what happened to Mrs. Pierce?"

"Very disturbing," Jasmine agreed as she sliced another sample. "When Detective Ferguson stopped here on Saturday morning, he asked me all sorts of questions."

Tess accepted the second chunk of fudge. "Even worse, Jasmine, he returned to Julie's that afternoon and accused her of involvement in Sylvia's fall from that platform."

Jasmine sputtered, "Well, he's way off base. Julie and I are friends. I can't imagine her harming anyone, no matter how much a person deserves it."

That last comment brought Gwen up short, so she said, "Sounds like you didn't like Sylvia."

"I'd never set eyes on her until she barged into Julie's party, so I have no personal opinion about the woman one way or the other. But after the three of you joined her husband on his search, the rest of us talked about Sylvia.

For the next few minutes, Gwen and Tess encouraged Jasmine to share that gossip, none of it flattering.

Finishing the fudge sample, Gwen said, "We'll take a pound of this Rocky Road… it's delicious."

"I knew you'd like it." Jasmine weighed the fudge. "You know, Sylvia never visited my booth or bought my fudge. If her death was not an accident, I have no idea who would have wanted her gone." Jasmin paused for only a split second. "Is that why you two are still on Nantucket? To support Julie until this whole mess gets sorted out?"

Impressed by Jasmine's analysis, Gwen answered, "Yes. Knowing her potential legal predicament, we decided to stay a while longer."

The young woman volleyed her glance between the sisters as she handed Gwen the white paper bag. "Be sure to come back while you're still on the island."

"We'll keep that in mind," Tess said, nudging Gwen. "Ready to check out the other booths?"

Sensing that Tess was anxious to depart, Gwen added the bag of fudge to her canvas sack. "Sure."

Waving goodbye to Jasmine, Tess pulled Gwen past several vendor booths until they were well down the row.

Gwen grasped Tess's sleeve. "Why the hurry?"

Tess shook her head. "I'm not sure. Something about Jasmine didn't sit right with me."

Seated in the Jeep, they quickly updated the tapestry journal before maneuvering the back roads to Sconset.

Chapter Thirty-Two

… late afternoon, Tuesday

"We're back," Gwen called, entering ahead of Tess.

Ursula strolled in from the kitchen, drying her hands on a leaf-themed towel, peering into their market sacks. "Nice selection. I'll prepare some of these for dinner."

Hearing footsteps, Gwen side stepped into the foyer to see Ben approach from the living room, Julie hobbling by his side. For a nano second, the green monster pricked Gwen's heart. With no claims on Ben, she pursed her lips and ignored her jealousy. "Hi, Ben. Didn't realize you were here. Your police sedan isn't parked out front."

"Hello, Gwen, Tess. My car is parked in the sandy lot past the corner where the bluff erosion begins. I walked here for a second chat with Julie about her security camera."

Gwen suspected there was more to his reason for being here, but given that Julie and Ursula were listening, she didn't press Ben for more details.

Ursula caught Ben's eye. "Staying for dinner?"

"I appreciate another invite, but no. I'm still avoiding conflict-of-interest."

He turned to Gwen. "Haven't seen you since our lunch on Sunday. How about you walk me to my car?"

Ben's statement was true. Though they'd talked on the phone, Gwen hadn't *seen* him until that very moment.

"You're parked past the protected end of the bluff walk?" Julie confirmed as she ushered them to the patio door and slid it open. "The erosion is quite dramatic from that corner if it's visible this late in the day."

After crossing the lawn, Gwen and Ben turned left onto the dirt path before she stole a look back at Julie's slider.

"She's watching us, Ben."

He didn't respond but kept walking until they passed the neighbor's hedge, holding aside a branch that poked into the pathway. "She's picking up on my fondness for you." Reaching for Gwen's hand, Ben squeezed. "Thanks again for being my C.I. out here. We make a good team."

Though comforted by his touch, Gwen's personal battle raged non-stop between her affection for the human Ben and her deep love for Parker's spirit waiting on the other side.

Not wanting to overreact, she said, "Sorry I haven't uncovered a clue that points you at the guilty person."

"All details are useful, Gwen. And, like you've said several times, there may not be a guilty person."

On the pretext of retrieving a tissue from her jeans pocket, Gwen pulled her hand from Ben's grasp, then said, "Did Officer Bryce have any luck obtaining security footage from Julie's neighbors?"

"Three so far. Some of the owners weren't home."

"Have the recordings revealed anything useful?"

"By the timestamps, early images of Sylvia before she knocked on Julie's slider, plus later images of Wyatt walking the path as he approached Julie's during his search. In between, quite a few women and men watching the storm. Logan printed the identifiable faces, plus pulled DMV photos of all the party guests. As we obtain more security footage and canvas other bluff residents, we'll ask if they recognize anyone as being on the bluff Friday night."

"But no footage of Sylvia on Julie's platform?"

"Not yet," Ben answered, his tone sullen. "If only Julie's security system had been working..."

"You asked her about it this afternoon?"

"I did. She plans to replace the old system. But that's not going to help us now."

"Do you think she turned it off intentionally?"

"Based on the timeline you shared, I doubt she had a chance before following Sylvia outside."

Lost in their thoughts and surrounded by the sound of the surf plus the salty evening air. neither one spoke as they continued walking.

Arriving at the fence that blocked further progress along the disappearing northern section of the bluff walk, Ben shared Logan's explanation that storm erosion had eaten into the path that used to exist ahead of them.

"Mother Nature is not always kind," Gwen said.

Turning left, they followed the grassy path along the fence to Baxter Road, arriving at the sandy parking lot.

As Ben approached his driver's side door, he quickened his step, turned around, and took a stance in front of Gwen. "I'm aware you've cooled toward me. I've let our police chief hijack my days and nights. When we return to Harbor Falls, I'll put a stop to his requests."

Gwen was well aware of Ben's hopes for them as a couple when his retirement time was finally his own. She could only cross her fingers that he'd forgotten her hospital quip back in June. He'd mentioned his possible marriage proposal. In her medicated state, she'd said never in her jinxed backyard, where a family wedding had been so disturbingly interrupted. Wrong joke for sure.

Though dusk approached, enough light remained for Gwen to see the affection in Ben's grey eyes and said, "Let's talk about all that after we've returned to Harbor Falls."

Ben straightened. "You're right. Nantucket during this investigation is not the place or the time." He glanced toward the setting sun. "You'd better hurry back to Julie's before she assumes this was more than a friendly walk. If she asks questions, don't reveal you've partnered with me."

A bit stung by his unnecessary warning, Gwen controlled her irritation. "I'm always careful to guard my C.I. status, Ben. Only Tess knows about our official arrangement."

"Sorry, Gwen. Didn't mean to insult you."

"Do you still consider Julie a person of interest?"

His shoulders lifted and dropped. "I haven't ruled her out completely, but it's seeming less and less likely."

Tilting his head down, Ben kissed Gwen's cheek.

Without reacting, she opened his car door, swinging it wide for him to drop behind the wheel.

He rolled down the window. "Good night, Gwen."

"Good night to you, too, Ben. Tess and I will share the results of today's activities when we call you later tonight."

When he nodded, she leaned closer. "What is Maeve cooking for you tonight?"

A Cheshire cat grin brightened his expression. "She promised me Shepherd's pie."

Chapter Thirty-Three
… late afternoon, Tuesday

After Ben's taillights faded, Gwen reversed her direction and walked quickly toward Julie's cottage in the diminishing light.

Without warning, the failure of Parker's spirit to appear during Sunday's follow-up séance drifted into Gwen's mind. She'd been troubled by his no-show then and was equally troubled now.

Was Ursula correct that the waters of the Nantucket Sound might have created a barrier to Parker's ghostly appearances?

Or had Gwen's understandable enjoyment of Ben's human companionship fractured her link to Parker?

When she crossed the lawn of Julie's cottage, the patio light blinked on, bathing the area in the same orange glow as the Halloween party, chasing away Gwen's unanswerable questions like smoke from the séance candles.

At the sound of the slider opening, she lifted her head to see Julie standing in the opening with her booted foot lifted like a flamingo, silhouetted by the light from the living room lamps.

"Did you enjoy your walk?" she asked.

Assuming Julie was curious about her conversation with Ben, Gwen deflected the third degree by asking, "Should you be walking on that ankle?"

Julie pointed at her support boot. "It's feeling better."

'Feeling better' was not 'back to normal,' so Gwen waved toward the couch. "Let's sit."

Julie hobbled over and rested her foot on the coffee table.

Settling on the end cushion and tucking one foot beneath her, Gwen asked, "Are you concerned about the bluff erosion?"

With a one-shoulder shrug, Julie replied, "The real estate agent informed me that three to four feet disappear each year. Eventually, I'll have to either move this cottage to the inland end of my lot across Baxter Road or sell my home outright."

"That's disheartening."

"I was aware of the threat before I purchased this property, but seashore homes are still in demand." She paused, then said, "When Ben stopped by earlier, he asked about my security system. When I told him it's never worked, he explained it might have recorded Sylvia on my platform Friday night."

Gwen scanned the area. No Ursula. No Tess. No noise echoing from the kitchen. Confused and a bit tense, Gwen responded, "Because you're the closest to it, I expect he's right about that."

"I could kick myself for not replacing the entire security system when I first moved in."

Unsure why Julie was confiding her conversation with Ben, Gwen waited to hear what she'd say next.

As expected, Julie continued, "Ben also asked why Wyatt chose me to help search for Sylvia."

Gwen was curious herself. "What did you tell him?"

Julie flicked her hand, implying the answer was of no consequence. "I simply explained that the residents along the bluff are … were… not particularly fond of Sylvia. I'd guess Wyatt assumed none of them would help him, so he didn't bother to ask."

"That makes perfect sense."

Julie leaned closer. "Does Ben know I asked you to chat with my party guests? I'd hate him to think I don't trust his detective skills."

Taking care to conceal her partnership with Ben, Gwen provided only a partial answer. "He did ask if I'd spoken to any of your friends since the party."

"And what did you tell him?"

"Each guest was surprised you're considered a person of interest and didn't believe you could harm anyone."

Julie leaned sideways and threw her arms around Gwen. "Thank you for telling me. I feel so much better. Did you visit any of them today?"

A bit uncomfortable with Julie's unexpected outpouring of emotion, Gwen said, "Tess and I chatted with Hester."

"Tell me about your time with dear Hester."

During Gwen's recap of the museum tour, she extended Hester's invitation for Julie to visit the portrait gallery and view the earlier likeness of Captain Tiffin.

"How exciting. I'll do that as soon as this ankle heals."

The sound of the front door opening caught Gwen's attention but didn't seem to surprise Julie.

Seconds later, Tess poked her head into the living room. "Hi, Gwen. Ursula and I are back from exploring the southern section of Sconset. Thanks for your suggestion, Julie. I'll help Ursula prepare dinner and let you know when it's ready."

"Thanks, Tess," Julie said. "I need to pay a few bills."

"And I need to freshen up," Gwen added.

Half an hour later, all four women raved about the crockpot chicken pasta plus sauteed zucchini.

When Tess's eyes drooped, she said, "I don't know about you, sis, but I'm heading to bed."

Gwen gathered her place setting. "It's been a busy day for both of us. I'm right behind you."

Ursula took possession of Gwen's dirty plate. "I'll clean up. Gotta earn my room and board."

***

Ben's voice answered during the second ring. "Long time, no hear," he joked. "Are we on speaker?"

"Not tonight," Gwen said. "Tess wore herself out walking with Ursula through southern Sconset with Ursula. She's already snoring."

"Am not," Tess yelled over from her bed. "Tell Ben good night for me."

"I heard her," he said. "Now, tell me the details of your interviews today. Who did you visit first?"

"That would be Hester at the historical society. She's a researcher who met Julie during her probe into the history of her cottage." Gwen shared the Whaling Museum tour, ending with Hester's invitation for Julie to view the earlier portrait of Captain Percy Tiffin.

"That'll be a good distraction for Julie," Ben commented. "What's your personal opinion of Hester?"

"For one, she's a soft-spoken senior citizen transplanted from England," Gwen answered. "Tess and I can't imagine her harming a fly. She invited us to lunch but provided no leads to a party guest who might have disliked Sylvia."

"I'll make note of that. Anyone else today?"

"Yes. Here's the conversation we had with Jasmine at the farm stand where she works." Gwen proceeded to read her notes to him before saying, "Tess was uneasy with her reactions and comments but couldn't quite determine why."

"Then I'll make a note to visit her officially. You and Tess will chat with your final two guests tomorrow?"

"That's the plan. Rose and Sandy. Both of them work in Nantucket proper."

"If you have a chance, let me know your results as soon as you're finished. I'll be interviewing Molly and possibly this Jasmine, and I want to provide a report to Ferguson."

His voice softened as though contemplating. "Who are we missing with means, motive, and opportunity?"

"What if," Gwen began, "Sylvia avoided Wyatt during his search and was still wandering the bluff after the party ended? As each guest left the party, she had a second opportunity to bump into Sylvia. Any of them holding a grudge against Sylvia could have tangled with her on that platform."

"It's possible we've misread the relationships between Julie and her friends," Ben suggested. "Also, if Sylvia *was* pushed to her death, the culprit could have been someone totally unconnected to Julie's party."

"Or no one at all," Gwen offered once again.

"Let's think about all these people overnight and talk again tomorrow. I wish you and Tess a solid night of sleep."

"And the same for you, Ben."

"Sweet dreams, Gwen."

Chapter Thirty-Four
… early morning, Wednesday

The previous evening, after savoring Maeve's Shepherd's Pie, Ben had wandered her Madaket neighborhood.

In the crisp November air, he mentally reviewed his investigation. Bottom line… he *still* had no definitive evidence to share with Jake Ferguson the next day.

When he returned to the quiet guest house, he'd left a note on Maeve's kitchen counter. *'If possible, I'd be grateful for a 7am breakfast. If I'm overstepping, I'll eat breakfast out.'*

That next morning, when he bounded down the stairs, steaming chipped beef gravy on toast plus a dish of sliced fresh pears awaited him on her dining room table.

Maeve herself appeared in the kitchen door. "Is your breakfast offering satisfactory, Mr. Snowcrest?"

"More than satisfactory. One of my favorites. Thanks for cooking before your usual breakfast hour." He stopped talking and forked another mouthful.

"My pleasure. Will you need lunch or dinner today?"

Ben didn't want to push his luck with the kindly guest house owner and great cook, so said, "Thanks for offering, Maeve, but not today. Perhaps I'll play tourist and sample one of the fine restaurants of Nantucket. I'll return this evening."

Retreating to his room, he collected his briefcase, hurried to his loaner, and drove to the police station.

***

Gwen glanced across Julie's table. "Are you sure you don't need your Jeep today? Tess and I are perfectly happy with our Uber driver."

Julie waved off Gwen's concern. "My ankle prevents me from doing much of anything. You and Tess are welcome to use my Jeep. What are your plans for today?"

"We're hoping to catch up with the last of your party guests, Rose then Sandy. More exploring," Tess answered. "But first, I need the bathroom. Be right back."

As Tess bounded up the staircase, Ursula gathered the breakfast dishes and carried them to the kitchen.

Julie looked over at Gwen. "You haven't uncovered any obvious clues about Sylvia's drowning?"

"I'm sorry. I'm a bit disappointed myself."

"Don't apologize, Gwen. If I'd replaced my security system, it might have recorded whatever happened at that platform on Friday night."

"If your camera had been *focused* on that platform," Gwen pointed out. "There's no way to second guess."

"You're right," Julie said. "If Ben obtains security footage from my neighbors, he might find some useful recordings."

Gwen could offer only a logical opinion. "He'll be crossing his T's and dotting his I's, so, if a recording of your platform exists, I wouldn't be surprised if Ben finds the footage."

"I'm hoping Detective Ferguson rules Sylvia's death an accident. I honestly hate the thought of anyone doing harm to another human – or animal for that matter," Julie said as she tossed her napkin to the table. "Nature calls, Gwen. The keys to the Jeep are on the foyer table. You can tell me about your day when you get back. See you and Tess later."

Gwen headed upstairs to collect her sister.

***

At the police station, after the officer inside the reception booth waved Ben through without double-checking his credentials, he rode the elevator to the second floor and made his way to the A/V office.

"Good morning, Logan."

"Same to you, Ben. I've already loaded the most recent security recording and did a quick review."

Opening his briefcase, Ben located the DMV photo of Addie Ferguson and tilted it for Logan to see.

"Did you notice her in this latest recording?"

"Addie? No. But we can take another look together."

After the footage was reset to the beginning, they both squinted at the images crawling across the monitor.

"I didn't see her," Ben commented, partially relieved.

"Me neither," Logan concurred. "But different cameras are set at different sensitivity levels, so she might show up in a recording we don't have yet."

"Or in the three SD cards we returned the other day. Pull up your copies, and we'll double check."

Seeing no Addie, Ben downplayed her as a likely suspect. Jake Ferguson would have been devastated.

"When will you return this newest disc to the mystery buff's neighbor?"

"This morning. And I want you to go with me again. We'll interview the storm watcher at the southern end of the bluff walk plus check residents who weren't home yesterday."

Returning the single disk to the machine, Logan made a copy for the police file, then popped the disk out and handed it to Ben, who dropped it into a fresh manila envelope, again noting the house number.

"Cross your fingers, Logan. I'll find Ferguson about you joining me again in Sconset. If we have any chance of uncovering what happened with Sylvia on Julie's platform, we need to locate additional security cameras. I'll text you when I'm ready to leave."

Out in the hallway, Ben spotted Jake Ferguson rushing into his office at the far end. Arriving at the open door, he noticed the detective pacing and paused before knocking.

Jake whirled around. "Oh, Ben. Listen, I apologize for jumping down your throat yesterday. I should leave my personal problems at home where they belong."

Pulling the visitor chair up close, Ben rested his forearms on the front edge of Jake's desk. "If you need a sounding board, I'm a good listener."

"You mentioned when you first arrived that you were married decades ago."

Ben grimaced. "We married too young. Do you want to tell me what's going on?"

Jake strode to his office door and closed it, returning to his chair and leaning back at a dangerous angle. "You sound like a shrink, but I'll tell you. Something's going on with Addie, and she won't tell me what's bothering her."

Ben recalled his interview with Jake's wife and the visitor Addie hadn't invited into the house. "How long ago did you notice her change in attitude?"

"Hard to say. Months, if I had to put a date stamp on it. I blame myself because I've been working too much and leaving Addie to entertain herself. She's got friends, of course, but a wife needs her husband's attention."

Ben glanced down at his crossed arms, waiting for Jake to gather his thoughts and add more detail.

A heavy sigh emanated from the detective. "Last night, I got home late for supper again and nearly tripped over her luggage at the front door."

"Did you know she was planning a trip?"

"Only after she reminded me she'd signed up for a seminar on the mainland with her volunteer group. My forgetfulness didn't improve her mood. I need to get my act together, Ben."

Had Addie been having an affair with Wyatt Pierce? Sylvia focused her suspicion on Julie because she would never have suspected her friend Addie. The fact that neither Ben nor Logan had spotted her on the recordings during Friday night's storm didn't eliminate Addie as the other woman.

Not used to advising other men, Ben said to Jake. "How about a marriage counselor?"

Jake popped his chair forward, mimicking Ben's crossed arms. "Sorry, I've taken us way off business. Did you stop by for a reason?"

Relieved that the marital issues were pushed to the side for the moment, Ben replied, "You're aware Logan and I obtained some security footage from a few bluff residents and some of the timestamped faces have been identified?"

At Jake's nod, Ben continued. "He and I need to continue knocking on doors k and hopefully get our hands on more recordings. I've heard that many of the bluff residents didn't like Sylvia. One of them could have held a grudge."

Jake scrubbed his face where stubble darkened his skin. "Are you suggesting someone besides Julie Robinson, or one of her guests, may have pushed Sylvia down those steps?"

"Just tossing out an alternate possibility, Jake. There's no evidence or eyewitnesses against anyone. What we need is footage that includes that platform on Friday night. A tragic slip and fall is still a distinct possibility."

"And you'd like to borrow Patrolman Bryce again?"

Ben nodded. "You did volunteer his assistance."

Jake waved off the reminder. "You're right. I did. So off with you. Bring me something solid, Ben."

Chapter Thirty-Five

… mid-morning, Wednesday

As Gwen drove them from Sconset into the town of Nantucket, she kept one eye on traffic as she glanced over at Tess. "I know you've been hoping we'd stumble on a clue to lead Detective Ferguson away from Julie, but so far nothing we've uncovered will point him at someone else."

"I know, I know," Tess said, her tone reflecting her disappointment. "All we can do is chat with these last two guests and see if they offer any other options."

Tess studied the notated guest list and Gwen's marked-up map, both resting on her lap. "Sandy works a few streets over from Rose, so we can walk from one to the other."

After maneuvering into a parking space, the sisters found their way to the first address and entered a gift shop. Tess nodded toward the young woman restocking a section of island mementos and mouthed, "There's Rose."

Gwen pretended to browse the knickknacks, stopping short when she bumped into Rose.

"Oh, I'm sorry. I should watch where I'm wandering."

Rose touched a shelf to rebalance herself. "That's okay. Shoppers jostle me all the time. I guess I'm invisible." Then she gazed first at Gwen, and then at Tess.

"Haven't I met you two somewhere recently?"

"I doubt it," Tess tossed back. "We only arrived last Friday for a Halloween party."

"That's it!" Rose exclaimed, then covered her mouth when other shoppers glanced her way. "You were both at Julie's house on Friday night."

Faking surprise, Gwen said, "That's right. Now I remember you. The '20's flapper, right? We didn't get a chance to chat during the party."

"No, we didn't," Rose agreed. "So much of your evening was taken up searching for that Sylvia woman."

Gwen leaned closer and whispered the question she'd asked all the other guests. "Wasn't it awful that she drowned near Julie's section of the bluff that same night?"

"Yes," Rose answered. "A detective stopped by here on Saturday morning and asked me about Sylvia showing up at the party."

"Unfortunately," Gwen continued, "that detective thinks Julie was involved."

Rose's expression revealed genuine shock. "That can't be true. Julie's one of the gentlest people I know."

The rest of the subtle exchange proceeded like most of the others. Rose didn't point her finger at any of the party guests and contributed nothing new to the mystery of Sylvia's tumble from the platform.

Concluding their visit by purchasing island trinkets for Jenna and Liz, Gwen ushered Tess from the shop.

They strode along the street in silence until Tess spoke. "Well, that was another fruitless conversation. One guest left."

***

After Logan drove them into Sconset, Ben indicated an open parking space near a sandwich shop on the other side of the small-scale roundabout.

Because Logan knew his way around this section of Sconset, Ben followed him onto the southern end of the Bluff Walk. They soon arrived at the home of a storm watcher identified in the security footage close-ups.

"My husband's not here at the moment," said the woman who answered their knock. "May I help you?"

After Ben explained their purpose and held out Sylvia's DMV photo, the wife said, "Sorry, but I don't recognize her. We did pass that platform during Friday's storm, but I don't recall seeing this woman." She handed it back.

When Logan asked if they could borrow the SD card from the security camera, she popped it out and handed it to him. "We rarely view the recordings, so keep it as long as you need to. And good luck."

When she closed the door, the lock clicked into place.

More good luck when they knocked on the door of the second identified storm watcher.

An elderly gentleman waved them into his living room. "What can I do for you fellas?"

Ben explained that he'd been recognized on a neighbor's security camera.

"Yes, I was out there waiting for the rain to arrive. The storms can be quite exciting if you're above the beach."

For the second time, Ben held up the copy of Sylvia's license photo. "Did you see this woman on the bluff?"

The old man peered at the picture. "Isn't this the carpenter's wife? She stumbles by here on a regular basis, but I don't recall seeing her Friday night."

When Logan asked about a security camera, the old man pooh-poohed the thought. "I'm an old geezer, and those new-fangled electronic gadgets are way above my paygrade. Sorry I haven't been much help."

***

By late-morning, with only a single new SD disk in hand, Logan drove them back to the station.

"I'm not holding out much hope that our luck will change with this latest recording, Logan, but take a look. I'm going into town to re-interview one or two of the party guests."

Settling in his sedan, Ben drove into Nantucket and located the Island Textiles shop.

When the bell jangled, a hefty woman looked up from a pile of linens. "Can I help you find something, sir?"

Ben saw no reason to delay his interview. "Maybe after we talk. Are you Molly Burns?"

Her expression hardened. "Yes. And who might you be?"

Ben stepped closer, extending his business card as he introduced himself. "Benjamin Snowcrest. I'm investigating a drowning over in Sconset on Friday night."

Molly squinted at his card, then stared at Ben. "Your address is on the mainland. By what authority are you involving yourself in a tragedy out here on our island?"

Ben switched to what he considered his most official voice. "Detective Jake Ferguson of the Nantucket Police Department requested my help with this case."

"Oh, I see," Molly said, her tone still skeptical. "And just what do you think I can contribute?"

"I understand you attended a Halloween party at the home of Julie Robinson the night of the drowning."

Molly's eyes narrowed. "That's correct."

"I also understand everyone left the party one by one."

"What does that matter?" she snapped.

Ben ignored Molly's obvious resistance to a detective from off-island. He held up Sylvia's photo. "Are you acquainted with Sylvia Pierce?"

With only a fleeting glance, Molly replied, "Only marginally. She's bought a few linens from me over the years. And she stopped by Julie's during the party."

"Are you aware that Sylvia Pierce is the woman who drowned Friday night?"

"Yes, I am."

"When you left the party, did you notice Mrs. Pierce on the platform beyond Ms. Robinson's lawn?"

Molly shook her head in sharp jabs. "No."

"Did you bump into her on the bluff walk pathway as you walked toward your car?"

"I was in a hurry before the rain circled back, so I paid no attention to anyone else who was fool enough to stand out there during a storm."

"Do you know her husband Wyatt Pierce?"

"Everyone knows Wyatt," she snapped. "He's the best carpenter on the island."

If she was happy that Sylvia was dead and hoping for Wyatt's attention, Molly wasn't about to reveal any of that, especially to outsider Ben.

He thanked her and left without browsing her displays, none the wiser for the interview but keeping an open mind.

His lack of success in resolving Sylvia Pierce's death made Ben question his detecting edge. Or was there nothing sinister to discover?

If Ben didn't report solid evidence to Jake Ferguson and soon, he'd no doubt be released from the case and sent packing on the ferry back to the mainland.

Bothered by the possibility, Ben slowly walked toward his loaner, stopping short at the sight of Julie's green Jeep parked on the opposite side of the cobblestoned street.

With no idea if Julie had driven into town herself or if she'd loaned her Jeep to Ursula, or even Gwen and Tess, he settled on a nearby bench, watched, and waited.

His patience was rewarded when he spotted the sisters approaching. He hopped up from the bench and cupped his hands on each side of his mouth before calling their names.

Both heads shot up.

Waving, Ben waited until a car and a delivery truck rumbled past before hustling across the uneven cobblestones. "Fancy meeting you here. Any success with your final two guests?"

Tess waved backwards in the direction of the gift shop they'd just exited. "Rose didn't have anything to add."

"Our last guest is a few streets over," Gwen finished.

Ben glanced at his watch. "How about an early lunch before you visit her?"

Gwen elbowed Tess and grinned. "We know a perfect place not far from where we're standing."

Chapter Thirty-Six

… early afternoon, Wednesday

Gwen swallowed the last bite of her grilled cheddar with tomato at the old pharmacy's lunch counter. Wiping her lips and fingers with a napkin, she glanced toward the back of the store, spotted the sign for the restrooms, and hopped down from the stool. "Gotta wash my hands. I'll be right back."

Ben half-swirled his stool to face Tess. "I'm sorry your trip to Nantucket turned sour."

"Not your fault," she responded. "I just wish Gwen and I could have uncovered something… anything… that would point Detective Ferguson away from Julie."

"Even the best detectives can't find clues that don't exist," Ben said. "The two of you are doing what you can."

Tess emptied her water glass. "Thanks for saying that. Sandy is our last interview."

As Tess spoke, Gwen came up beside them, re-claiming her stool on Ben's other side. "I share Tess's misgivings. Unless you can suggest another direction for us, our usefulness to you will end today."

Ben retrieved his credit card to pay for their lunches. "Let's not give up until all three of us have turned over every stone we can find."

Tess said, "If you're waiting for Julie to confess that she pushed Sylvia from that platform, she hasn't."

"Most criminals don't," Ben said, signing the charge slip and tucking the copy into his wallet. "I'm on my way to chat with Jasmine at the farm stand, and then returning to the station to catch up with Logan and Jake. Call me after you speak with the final guest, Gwen." He waved to the sisters and exited the old pharmacy.

***

Linking arms with Tess, Gwen hustled them along two streets and into the print shop where Sandy Owens worked.

Gwen worried she hadn't been dedicated enough to removing Julie as a person of interest. Her mystery solving in Harbor Falls had been based on personal goals to prove innocent a friend who'd been wrongly accused of a crime.

But Julie, Tess's long-ago college roommate, was a virtual stranger to her. Had Gwen been as diligent as she should have been? Had she been clever enough during their chats with the party guests? Had she missed clues dropped unknowingly by one of Julie's friends?

To take herself off the hook, Gwen entertained the idea that maybe no one could – or should – be blamed for Sylvia's drowning. Accidental slip and fall remained an extremely viable option. Not wanting to upset Tess, Gwen didn't give voice to any of these musings.

Entering the print shop, the sisters were told Sandy was off-island and would be back first thing the next morning.

Deflated by yet another delay, Gwen and Tess headed back to Julie's place.

***

At the police station, Ben bounded up the front stairs to the second floor and knocked on the doorframe of Jake's office.

The man's head jerked up and he gestured Ben to enter. "Did you and Patrolman Bryce discover any revealing images in those security recordings?"

Ben lowered himself into the guest chair. "We've identified Julie Robinson's friends by comparing faces to the DMV photos, but so far, no incriminating activity."

"Anything come of Gwen and Tess's party guest visits?"

"Nothing that points to another potential suspect."

Jake sat back in his chair. "You're telling me you haven't made any progress?"

"Not yet, Jake. Gwen and Tess are planning on one more casual interview this afternoon."

With a quick move, Jake jerked his chair upright and leaned across his desk. "Based on what you haven't uncovered, Ben, I'm certain Julie Robinson either disposed of Sylvia before rejoining her guests in her studio or waited until all her friends had gone home before tracking down the woman out on the bluff and coaxing her to that platform to do her in."

"There's no proof for either scenario," Ben objected.

Jake flicked his hand in dismissal. "Very convenient that Ms. Robinson's camera wasn't working. Did you confirm it's inoperable or simply take her word for it?"

Jake's skepticism cut Ben to the quick. He'd expected at least understanding from a fellow detective.

Controlling the anger in his voice, Ben said, "I checked Julie's ancient security set-up, and it appeared inoperable. When I pointed out that a recording from her patio aimed at the platform could have proved what really happened to Sylvia Pierce that night, Julie appeared truly regretful that she hadn't replaced the old system."

Jake simply harrumphed but said nothing.

Ben continued, "I also mentioned to you the other day that I overheard a conversation between Wyatt Pierce and Julie. There were no romantic words, and I didn't sense a motive from either of them to eliminate his wife."

Jake left his chair and paced. "How about this for a motive? Julie Robinson had developed a crush on Wyatt during her renovation. Realizing he wasn't interested, she took advantage of the opportunity provided by that storm to get rid of his alcoholic wife, hoping that would free him to be more open to her advances."

"Your imagination is out of control, Jake. Are you saying their affair hadn't yet begun in spite of Sylvia's accusation?"

Ben resisted the urge to suggest that Wyatt's affair could be with Jake's own wife Addie. Had Wyatt ridden the morning ferry to the mainland with her?

Not uttering that possibility to Jake, Ben said, "How about I revisit Wyatt and pin him down about why Sylvia thought he was having an affair with Julie?"

"You're delaying the obvious, Ben, but go ahead and grill the man. And while you're in his neighborhood, take a closer look at Ms. Robinson's security camera."

A knock interrupted their tension.

They both turned to see Patrolman Bryce standing at the open door, looking like a kid caught with his hand in the cookie jar. "Sorry to intrude, but I have an update from our most recent security footage."

"What did you find?" Jake demanded.

"A recording of the search party and then Wyatt continuing north. A half hour later, a second recording of him hurrying in the opposite direction toward his home."

Jake headed for the door. "That proves nothing, but let's have a look."

In the A/V office, the three men peered at the images as Logan moved from one frame to the next.

"Like I said, that doesn't prove anything," Jake blustered. "Nothing more specific, Patrolman Bryce?"

Sensing Logan's discomfort, Ben rushed to answer, "We haven't found any other neighbors' cameras that were directed toward the platform in front of Julie's house, so no recordings of Sylvia, either by herself or with someone else. We're still hoping to come across additional footage."

"Did you collect the security footage from Ms. Robinson's immediate neighbors on both sides?"

Logan replied, "Neither of them were home when we canvassed the bluff residents."

Ben added, "I've contacted a local real estate office about caretakers but haven't heard back."

Rummaging in his desk drawer, Jake held out a business card. "A friend of mine uses this property management group. If Ms. Robinson's neighbors hired these guys to keep an eye on their homes, they can contact the owners for permission to let you inside and commandeer the security tapes," Jake grumbled. "The camera focus of the people next door is more likely to include Ms. Robinson's platform."

Logan made a motion with his hand. "If I might add, sir, none of the residents who were out on the bluff that night that we've spoken to mentioned hearing a woman scream."

Jake jerked his head in Logan's direction. "Are you implying, Patrolman Bryce, that Mrs. Pierce did not utter a sound because she purposely threw herself down those steps?"

His face reddening, Logan answered, "Not at all, sir. I'm simply reporting an observation during our interviews. The noise of the storm could have covered her scream."

"Don't forget, Jake," Ben interjected, "we're still waiting for the coroner's final autopsy report. That might provide answers to explain Mrs. Pierce's final condition."

Chapter Thirty-Seven

… mid-afternoon, Wednesday

Returning to Julie's house from downtown Nantucket, Gwen entered ahead of Tess and popped her head into the kitchen. "Where's Julie?"

Ursula pointed upward. "In her studio. She's finally painting a seaside scene."

"Let's go up, Tess," Gwen said, already halfway to the staircase.

In the third-floor studio, they found Julie perched on the stool near her easel, facing out the dormer window. On the adjacent table, the paint tubes remained capped, brushes lingered, tips unsoiled, in the ceramic mug.

"Julie?" Tess called softly.

Her college roommate slammed her foot to the floor to keep from tumbling off the stool. "Oh, I didn't hear you come in."

"Sorry we startled you," Gwen said to Julie's back. "We bumped into Rose at the gift shop."

Julie spoke over her shoulder. "Did she tell you anything to convince Detective Ferguson I'm not his person of interest?"

Gwen recalled her own fear of arrest for the death of an uninvited houseguest years before, so understood Julie's sharp tone. "I'm afraid she didn't."

Without making eye contact with either sister, Julie reached sideways for an unblemished apron, and tied it around her waist. "I'm working on my first painting since college, so I'd appreciate some privacy."

Noting the blank canvas, Gwen glanced at Tess and pointed her chin toward the frosted door. Sliding it closed behind them, the sisters descended the staircase in silence.

When they reached the second floor, Tess whispered, "Julie isn't holding up well."

"That's obvious," Gwen said.

As they entered their guest suite, Tess turned toward the bathroom. "We've uncovered no one who could be blamed for Sylvia's death. How can Detective Ferguson call her drowning anything but a sad accident?" Tess's question remained unanswered as she closed their bathroom door.

Moving to the window, Gwen retrieved her cellphone.

***

"Gwen!" Liz shouted from her Harbor Falls bookshop. "Thanks for your texts, but hearing your voice is so much better. Have you flushed out the culprit? Are you returning to Harbor Falls soon?"

"Slow down, Liz," Gwen implored, "and I'll tell you."

For the next few minutes, Gwen recounted her unsuccessful attempts to find other persons of interest besides Julie.

"And what about Ben's efforts?" Liz asked.

"Equally non-productive."

"Will you, Tess, and Ben will be riding the ferry soon?"

"I'll let you know as soon as I do, Liz."

"Okay, I'll try to be patient. Jenna stopped in yesterday. She didn't say this aloud, but I think she's lonely. When she comes home from her classes, there's only your aloof cat. I sense she misses you terribly."

A twinge tugged at Gwen's heart. "I'll call her as soon as you and I hang up."

***

About to exit the A/V office, Jake turned back. "Patrolman Bryce, I need you in Madaket. A gang of teenagers are suspected of post-Halloween mischief." He handed over a thin manila folder. "There's not much detail in here. Drive over there and see what you can find out."

Walking beside Logan to the parking lot, Ben could tell by the young officer's jaunty step that he was excited by his first unofficial detective assignment, and said, "Good luck."

"Thanks, Ben. If I'm successful in Madaket, I'm hoping Detective Ferguson will promote me to the investigation unit."

Ben drove himself back to Sconset, parking at the central market across from the local bus stop. Striding north along the bluff, he stopped at the home where he and Logan had interviewed the owner's wife that morning.

The door was flung open by a man the stature and bulk of a football player. "You must be the cop who convinced my wife to hand over our security camera recording."

The wife stood a few feet behind him, lifting her shoulders as a sign of apology for her husband's rudeness.

Ben extended the envelope containing the SD disk. "We appreciated the opportunity to view your images. Thanks to you both for your cooperation."

As the door slammed shut behind him, Ben chalked up the exchange to a minor domestic dispute and continued his trek along the dirt path.

Ben walked north quite a distance until he knocked on Wyatt's porch door facing the bluff. He waited, then knocked again and waited some more. Either Wyatt wasn't inside or was ignoring Ben's knock.

Could the man have gone off-island with Addie as Ben envisioned when Jake mentioned her trip to the mainland?

Ben passed three more houses until he reached Julie's immediate neighbor to the south. Once again, no one answered the door.

By passing Julie's cottage, Ben repeated his knocking at the home on the northern side of the hedge where he'd crouched just the other day to eavesdrop on her conversation with Wyatt.

Once again discouraged, Ben reached into his pocket and pulled out the business card Jake had given him. He placed a call directly to the property management group, deflated when he was forwarded to the voicemail system. Hoping for a quick response, Ben left a detailed message about accessing the security systems in the homes on both sides of Julie's address.

And then he backtracked to Julie's patio and knocked.

Ursula approached, drying her hands on a kitchen towel before sliding the door open.

"Hello, Ben. Please come in." She moved aside, pointing down to remind him of the step-off onto the living room carpet. "Are you here to finally accept our invitation to dinner?"

He shook his head. "I still can't fraternize with any of you, although whatever you're cooking smells delicious."

Ursula preened, advising, "Goulash. Too bad you can't stay. If you're here to see Julie, she's up in her studio."

"Thanks. I'll let you get back to your stove."

She smiled at him. "Dinner won't be ready for a while yet if you change your mind." Turning on her heel, she hurried ahead of him, ducking through the kitchen arch.

Though Ben wondered if Gwen and Tess were inside the cottage, he needed to stay on topic, so headed up the staircase until he reached the third floor.

To be polite, Ben knocked on the frosted door before sliding it open. Julie sat near her easel with a paint brush held aloft, her foot propped atop an upholstered footstool.

Speaking over her shoulder, she called, "How am I supposed to paint if I'm constantly interrupted?"

Then she half-turned to identify the intruder, meeting Ben's eyes, her face falling. "Oh, it's you, Ben. Sorry."

"I see you're still wearing the ankle support. Is it still causing you pain?"

"Only when I walk on it. Why are you back, Ben?"

"I have a few questions."

Tossing the unused brush onto the empty palette, she glared at him. "Haven't I answered all your questions?"

"Just trying to wrap up the case."

She huffed. "Then ask your questions."

Ben didn't move any closer. "All right. Do you know if both of your immediate neighbors aren't home because they've closed up for the season?"

"I'm not close with either of them, so they don't share their comings and goings. Why do you ask?"

"Security cameras from either of those homes might include your platform. Maybe show Sylvia Pierce out there by herself on Friday night." He paused before saying, "You'd be off the hook with Detective Ferguson."

"And that would be a relief, Ben, but I can't help you."

Somehow, he'd expected her answer, so he broached his second topic. "While I'm here, can I take a closer look at your security system? You might not need to replace it if the problem is a broken wire that's easily fixed."

Not a master of electronics by any stretch of the imagination, Ben faked his expertise.

Julie slid off her artist stool and hobbled toward him, her blonde hair pulled off her face into a severe ponytail, her blue eyes hard.

"You're overstepping your authority, Ben. I've watched enough TV police dramas to know my rights. Apparently, seeing that the lights are not blinking is not enough to prove the system is not working. If you want to inspect my security set-up more thoroughly, you'll have to come back with an official search warrant."

She had him dead to rights.

Ben suspected obtaining a search warrant this late in the day wouldn't happen. "If that's the way you want to play this game, Julie, I'll be back."

His cell buzzed. Though Ben didn't recognize the number, it wasn't marked as spam, so he answered to find out who was trying to get in touch.

"Is this Ben Snowcrest?" asked the man.

Turning away from Julie, Ben lowered the volume of his voice. "Yes, that's me."

"I'm with the property management company. We've never failed to assist in an official investigation. We followed up on your voicemail request and spoke to the owners of those two properties in Sconset. They each gave permission to access their security system and borrow the recordings, but both insisted that you bring a search warrant."

Ben walked toward the frosted door, lowering his volume even further. "As it happens, I'll be obtaining a search warrant first thing tomorrow and will request these two as well."

"Good. Let us know when you're on your way to Sconset and we'll meet you at the southernmost address."

"I'll do that. Thank you." Ben disconnected.

Without another word to Julie, Ben turned on his heel, and hurried down the two flights of the staircase.

Through the archway into the kitchen, Ursula called, "Have you decided to stay for dinner, Ben?"

"Afraid not." He soon hurried south along the bluff walk.

Chapter Thirty-Eight
… early-morning, Thursday

"Not a problem that you need your Jeep today," Gwen assured Julie. "Tess and I have grown fond of our Uber driver. Are you sure you can drive with that ankle?"

Julie waved off the concern. "Ankle's much better. I'm not about to become a malingerer. Besides, my Jeep has an automatic transmission. My left foot is only sprained, but I can use my right for gas and brake."

Ursula came up beside them. "You know, Julie, I can drive you anywhere you need to go."

Patting her cousin's arm, Julie smiled. "I know you would. I want to drive alone with the windows down."

***

Entering the Clerk of the Court's office, Ben walked up to Logan. "Sorry to interrupt your Madaket investigation."

"It's a nuisance complaint, Ben. I'll get back to it after I request this warrant for you."

"I need two more."

Logan said, "Shouldn't be a problem."

With three search warrants in his pocket, Ben called the man at the property management group with an estimated ETA and drove back to Sconset.

About to pass Wyatt's home, a quick question niggled Ben, and he screeched to a stop.

Walking past the work truck in the street-side driveway, he touched the hood, this time finding it cold.

Still speculating that Wyatt might have fled Nantucket with Addie, Ben knocked. Thinking he heard movement inside, he knocked again.

When Wyatt opened the door, his red-rimmed eyes could not be ignored. Ben's theory about the man's escape on the ferry fluttered into the clear morning sky. Still, the fact that Wyatt remained in town didn't negate the possibility of an affair with Addie Ferguson. A perfect motive to rid himself of his drunken wife.

"Detective Snowcrest," Wyatt stated, his voice sullen.

Rather than pounce with his questions, Ben switched to a gentler approach. "I was in the neighborhood and thought I'd stop by to see how you're holding up."

"I'm finalizing funeral arrangements for my poor Sylvia if that gives you a clue." He stepped aside. "I'm sorry. Please come in. Do you have any news?"

Though Ben was usually a good judge of sincerity, he found Wyatt tough to read. "Nothing specific, but I need to ask a few delicate questions."

"Go ahead. Let's get this over with."

"Was your wife seeing a counselor of some sort?"

"If you mean for her drinking, no, and she refused to attend the AA meetings."

Ben shuffled his feet. "How about a psychiatrist?"

Wyatt's expression darkened. "What are you implying? Do you think my Sylvia was depressed and threw herself down those steps on purpose?"

Ben held firm. "We need to explore all avenues before we can close the case."

Wyatt's nostrils flared. "No counselors. No psychiatrists. No AA. My Sylvia was simply an insecure wife who assumed I had an affair with every woman I met." He stormed to his front door and whipped it open. "You can leave now."

Ben settled in his loaner and slammed the steering wheel with the palm of his hand. *Why was everyone being difficult?*

Then he patted the search warrants in his jacket pocket. His reputation as a detective rested on the sightline of the neighbors' security cameras.

He could only hope that the focus of one or both of them included Julie's platform. He had no other options to reveal the person standing on that platform with Sylvia.

Only then could Ben let Wyatt mourn his wife in peace.

***

As their Uber driver pulled to the curb at the printshop, Gwen said from the back seat, "What are our chances you can wait for us? We shouldn't be long."

The man leaned across the seat divide and grinned at them. "Sure. No other rider requests at the moment."

As the sisters clambered out, Gwen said to Tess. "Let's be up front with Sandy about why we're visiting her."

"Right. We can't justify walking in off the street."

A stern woman called Sandy, who quickly joined them.

"Hi. Are you the women who stopped here yesterday looking for me?"

"That's right," Gwen answered.

Sandy looked closer at their faces. "Weren't you at Julie's party last Friday night?"

"Good eye," Tess said, taking the lead. "We'll get right to the reason we wanted to speak to you. Are you aware of Sylvia Pierce's drowning on Friday night?"

Sandy nodded. "I am. A detective stopped by as I was leaving my house Saturday morning. I wasn't able to contribute much about that woman. I'd never met her until she barged through Julie's slider during the party."

Gwen took a turn. "Have you heard that the lead detective considers Julie a person of interest?"

Sandy's expression turned to shock. "That's outlandish. I only met her last spring, but she is a non-violent person. Is that why you're here? Gathering testimonials to convince the detective she's above suspicion?"

Tess answered, "You're very perceptive. We're hoping you can contribute something useful that the police missed."

"Has anyone else been helpful?"

"No one's suggested a person who may have wanted Sylvia out of the picture."

"Oh," Sandy murmured. "You mean someone besides Julie because of her having an affair with Sylvia's husband?"

242

"When you left the party, did you happen to see Sylvia on the platform not far from Julie's patio?"

"I left by the front door, so no. Why is that important?"

"We've been hoping to find someone who spotted Sylvia with another person out there."

Sandy's head wagged. "Sorry I can't help you."

The stern woman poked her head into the reception area and called to Sandy.

"I've got to get back to my project. Good luck. I'd hate to see Julie arrested if she's innocent." Turning, Sandy disappeared through the rear door.

Out the front entrance, Gwen and Tess bundled themselves into the back seat of the Uber car. Their driver zoomed along the main road toward Sconset and deposited them at Julie's front walkway.

As Gwen paid the man, Ursula rushed out the front door and down the steps. "I'm so glad you two are back. Did Julie tell you where she was going in her Jeep?"

"No, she didn't," Gwen answered. "Why?"

"She's not answering my texts or phone calls. She didn't even scribble a note. Since the day I arrived, she and I have been going everywhere together. This is not like her."

"Well," Gwen said in an effort to reassure Ursula, "she did mention wanting to drive alone with the windows down. But we'll check our phones."

Gwen and Tess retrieved their cell phones, shaking their heads after checking their own messages.

Tapping into other sections, Tess added, "No voicemail or email either."

Ursula led them inside and dropped into a dining room chair, resting her head in her hands. "She's been gone too long. I can't imagine why she hasn't returned."

"You said Ben was here yesterday," Gwen said. "Any idea what they discussed?"

"None. They were up in her studio until he rushed down the staircase and out the patio door. I'm really worried."

Chapter Thirty-Nine

… early afternoon, Thursday

Ben pulled into the parking area at Julie's neighbor to the south, next to an SUV with a magnetic Property Management sign on the side.

A man on the porch came down to greet Ben. "Can I see some identification, please."

"Of course," Ben answered, pulling out his license and business card, along with the search warrant.

Satisfied, the man opened the front door and waved Ben inside. Together, they located the security system panel and removed the SD card.

After repeating this same sequence at the house north of Julie's cottage, Ben thanked the man.

Those two recordings were more important than inspecting Julie's defunct security system. After calling Logan to meet him at the police station, Ben sped along to roads, anxious to view the footage immediately.

*****

"I just checked with the emergency dispatcher," Ursula stammered. "No accident with a green Jeep. The local hospital hasn't admitted her as a patient. I hope she's not lying in a ditch on a side road, and no one has spotted her."

Gwen's sleuthing experience kicked in. "Did Julie pack an overnight bag?"

Ursula shrugged. "I haven't checked."

Taking a step toward the staircase, Tess pointed up. "Let's have a look."

The three women rushed to the second-floor master suite.

Ursula quickly emerged from the walk-in closet shaking her head. "Her suitcase isn't here."

Though Gwen's mind whirled with multiple explanations, she guided the jittery Ursula to the nearest bed and sat down beside her. "We could be worrying about nothing. Has Julie made any offhand remarks that explain where she's gone?"

"None that I recall," Ursula moaned. "My sensitivities are limited to ghosts. I wish I could read minds."

Tess eased down on Ursula's other side. "Do you think Julie *was* involved in Sylvia's tumble and Ben's investigation is making her nervous?"

Ursula's eyes widened. "What makes you jump to that conclusion? When that Detective Ferguson showed up on Saturday afternoon and accused her, Julie was adamant she shouldn't be blamed."

Gwen came to Tess's rescue. "Did Julie tell you that Ben asked to inspect her security system?"

"No, she didn't mention it," Ursula glared at Gwen. "How do you know that?"

Deciding that Ursula's panic warranted relief, Gwen informed her that they'd had lunch with Ben the day before.

He'd told them that the security recordings from other bluff houses hadn't included images of the platform and that he planned to gain entry to the homes of the immediate neighbors, thumbing left then right to indicate the adjacent houses.

"So," Ursula began, "if there's a video that incriminates Julie, Ben just hasn't found it yet?"

Gwen answered with a nod. "And let's not forget Sylvia's suspicion that her husband Wyatt was having an affair with Julie. Do you think the two of them are escaping together?" Gwen's wild leap of a theory didn't matter if it eased Ursula's worry that Julie was lying in a ditch.

Ursula jumped to her feet and stared down at the sisters. "I don't know if any of your wild imaginings are true, but I'm calling Julie's cell again." Seconds later, she made a face and left another desperate voicemail, then typed out another text, finally turning to Gwen and Tess. "We need to find her."

Ursula rushed from the suite and down the staircase.

Gwen and Tess caught up with her as she flung open the front door. "Hold on, Ursula. We don't have a car."

"Then call your Uber driver," Ursula screamed.

"First," Gwen soothed, "I'm calling Ben."

***

Seeing the name on the caller ID, Ben answered immediately. "What's up, Gwen?"

"Julie's missing, along with her luggage."

"Damn," Ben responded. "She demanded a search warrant to check her security system. I hope she wasn't just stalling."

"That doesn't matter now, Ben. Where are you?"

"The property management group met me at both neighbors' houses to turn over the security footage. I'm on my way back to the station to take a look at the images."

"Did Julie know you were getting warrants for her neighbors' camera recordings?"

Ben paused to think. "Maybe. The call about permission from the owners buzzed in while I was about to leave her studio late yesterday."

"I hate to say it, Ben, but I think Julie's escaping."

"If she is, there are only two ways off the island. The airport or the ferry. Does she prefer one over the other?"

He listened as Gwen asked Ursula, then came back on the line. "Julie's never mentioned a preference."

"Then we'd better check both. I'm calling Detective Ferguson right now."

"Listen, Ben. Tess, Ursula, and I are stranded at Julie's unless our Uber driver is available."

"I'll head back your way. Call your Uber driver, but don't give him a destination until we talk again."

Disconnecting, Ben made a U-turn and stepped on the gas toward Sconset.

***

After Gwen shared Ben's instructions, she dialed their driver, quickly made a writing gesture, mouthing *pen.*

Ursula whipped open a kitchen drawer and extended a pad of paper along with a pencil.

Scribbling a phone number, Gwen ended the call and held up her note. "Our guy has been hired for the rest of the day, but he gave me this number for another driver." Dialing, Gwen left a voice message, then disconnected.

"So now we just wait?" Tess asked.

"We have no other option," Gwen answered. "If Ben gets here before we hear from the other Uber driver, we'll cancel our request. If the Uber driver calls before Ben arrives, we'll hire him, then stall if he gets here before Ben. We're stuck in a Catch-22 situation."

The waiting game began.

***

Answering after two rings, Jake barked, "What is it?"

"We've got movement on the Sylvia Pierce case."

"Well, don't beat around the bush, Ben. Tell me."

"Just got a call from Gwen. Julie Robinson drove away from her cottage without telling anyone where she was going, and her luggage is missing."

"Damn," Jake sputtered. "She's trying to escape. I'll hightail it over to the airport and instruct Patrolman Bryce to meet you four at the eastern ferry dock."

"I'm approaching Julie's house now to pick up Gwen, Ursula, and Tess."

"Good idea. If Ms. Robinson has chosen the ferry over the airport, let's hope she's spotted before she boards the next boat. If she's prevented from boarding, her cousin and friends should be a calming influence. Keep me informed, Ben."

Chapter Forty

… late afternoon, Thursday

As Ben's police loaner came to a stop at the entrance to the first ferry landing, a cruiser pulled alongside, its light spinning.

Through the open window, Logan Bryce called, "Ben, I got here as fast as I could. You can park right there."

Gwen, Tess, and Ursula scrambled out, and Ben introduced them to the patrolman.

The deafening blast of a ferry horn filled the air.

Logan scanned their faces. "I can't tell if that's approaching this dock or the next one. We'd better rush our search for Ms. Robinson at this one first."

Ben said, "We could be all wrong about her trying to flee Nantucket by boat."

"But you could be right," Logan said. "Let's go."

When none of them spotted Julie among the passengers lining up in the queue, they hurried back to the vehicles. Ben pointed at Logan's swirling cruiser light. "You might want to turn that off. If Julie's at the second dock, we don't want her diving into the harbor to keep us from catching up with her."

"Then let's hurry. Follow me, Ben. No matter where I park, pull in behind me." As Logan eased into traffic, the swirling light went dark.

Minutes later, they arrived at the other landing.

Gazing down the long dock, Ben took charge. "The right side appears to be benches and luggage trolleys. If Julie's here, she's trying to stay out of sight. Let's all stroll along the left side. Whoever spots Julie first, don't shout. Just give a wave to the rest of us."

Gwen and Tess took turns entering the shops and alleys while Ben, Ursula, and Logan moved through the crowd mulling about.

As they came to the empty slip where the ferry was slowing to pull up to the dock, Ursula bumped her elbow into Ben, pointing at the queue where passengers waited to board.

"See that woman with blonde hair threaded through the back of her baseball cap?" Ursula asked. "I recognize that ponytail. And watch, she's limping."

Ben called softly to Logan, Gwen, and Tess and gestured toward the pony-tailed woman who looked like Julie. "Any idea if she's armed?"

"I doubt it," Ursula replied. "Remember her reaction when she spotted your piece? She claimed she hates guns. And I can't imagine she thought to grab a kitchen knife before she drove away from her cottage."

"In that case, you three make your way over to that bench." He pointed to the opposite side of the dock. Logan and I will confirm she's Julie before we stop her from boarding."

At Ben's touch, the woman jerked away, then Julie stared at him, recognition darkening her expression.

"What are you doing here, Ben?"

"Fleeing Nantucket is not the answer, Julie."

When Ben and Logan gripped her arms and turned her around, Julie struggled, stiffening when she noticed Ursula, Tess, and Gwen watching.

Like a ragdoll, Julie sagged to the deck boards, sobbing. "I'm so sorry. I tried to save Sylvia. Really I did."

Lifting Julie to her feet, Ben and Logan settled her on the bench, taking care not to bump her ankle boot.

Behind them, Detective Jake Ferguson's voice boomed, "What's the situation, Patrolman Bryce?"

Logan indicated the sobbing Julie. "Ms. Robinson was about to board the ferry."

Jake peered down at the distraught Julie. "Ms. Robinson, didn't I ask you not to leave Nantucket while we investigated Sylvia Pierce's death?"

Raising her tear-streaked face, Julie said nothing.

Rather than wait to see how the situation would unfold, Ben sidled close to Jake, keeping his voice low. "Did you hear Julie say she tried to save Sylvia?"

"No, but it doesn't matter," Jake answered, reaching for Julie. "Ms. Robinson, you need to come with me to the station for questioning."

Ursula squatted before Julie and grasped her hands. "Don't say anything. I'll call a defense attorney I know."

"Defense attorney!" Julie swiped at her tears. "But I tried to stop her from falling."

Jake grunted. "Thank you for clarifying. Julie Robinson, you're under arrest for manslaughter and failure to report an accident." He recited the Miranda warning.

When Julie opened her mouth to speak, Ursula placed two fingers on her cousin's lips. "Shhh."

Jake turned to Ben. "Thanks for all your help."

Ben shook his head. "Gwen, Tess, and Ursula deserve much of the credit."

Jake tipped his cap to them. "Then I thank all four of you. I'll need a report, Ben."

Then Jake stared at Julie, "Ms. Robinson, if you promise not to make a scene, I won't cuff you."

At Julie's subtle nod, he grasped her arms and helped her up from the bench.

Turning to Logan, he commanded, "Patrolman Bryce, follow me and this prisoner to the station."

Looking down at Julie's ankle boot, Jake guided her slowly toward the other end of the dock.

Logan, Ben, Gwen, Tess, and Ursula followed.

Before they reached the entrance, Wyatt Pierce emerged from the crowd of onlookers and blocked their progress.

As new tears flowed down Julie's cheeks, she turned her face up to Wyatt's. "I'm so sorry. Sylvia's fall wasn't my fault. When she fainted, I tried to hold onto her clothing, but she slipped through my fingers."

When Jake nudged Julie forward, Wyatt took a stance beside Ben. "I know you suspected me of arranging my

Sylvia's drowning. Now you know I didn't. I can't believe Julie was involved."

"How did you know she was here?" Ben asked.

"My friend with a police scanner."

"It's a tragic situation for everyone," Ben said, placing a comforting hand on Wyatt's shoulder.

Wyatt said, "If you're here on Sunday afternoon, I've arranged a memorial for my Sylvia."

"If we're still on Nantucket, I'll certainly attend."

Wyatt nodded and walked off.

Ahead, Jake spread his hand atop Julie's head before easing her into the back seat of his SUV. He closed the door, then waved Ben to the side and lowered his voice.

"Addie's back home. I apologized to her for spending too much time at work. To be honest, Ben, I was wondering if Wyatt's affair had been with her, but she swore she's been faithful to me. I'm cutting my hours at the station. I think we're going to be okay."

"Glad to hear it, Jake. Too many marriages find themselves on the rocks these days. Adjusting your routine is a smart move. Good luck."

Nodding his agreement, Jake clapped Ben on his shoulder and dropped into the driver's seat.

Julie stared out the window as the police vehicles pulled into traffic, both sirens silent, soon disappearing from sight.

Ben drove Gwen back to the cottage.

Ursula located Julie's green Jeep and followed behind.

Chapter Forty-One

… early morning, Friday

After meeting Logan in the A/V office to view both neighbor's SD recordings before turning them over to Jake for the legal procedures, Ben drove to Julie's home and knocked, knowing full-well that she wasn't inside.

When Ursula opened the door, her forehead buckled with concern. "Come in, Ben. Do you think Julie's okay?"

"I was at the police station first thing this morning, but I wasn't allowed to talk to her. Jake assured me they made her comfortable, but I doubt she got much sleep."

Swiping his feet on the mat, he followed Ursula inside and sniffed the air. "Smells good."

"When I'm nervous, I bake," Ursula explained. "That's a double batch of cranberry muffins. There's plenty if you want to join us for breakfast."

Because Ben had skipped Maeve's breakfast, he gratefully followed Ursula into the dining room where Tess was pouring tea into a collection of cups.

When Gwen looked up at Ben, his heart fluttered. With little opportunity for personal time on Nantucket, he vowed to revive their connection, hoping to progress from friendship to something more substantial.

Gwen was the first to speak. "I was wondering if we'd see you again."

"I wasn't about to leave Nantucket before sharing the good news with the three of you."

"About Julie?" Ursula asked.

Ben nodded, lowering himself into an empty chair and reaching for a warm muffin.

"So, tell us already," Ursula demanded.

Swallowing, Ben began. "The property management group obtained permission from the owners of Julie's neighbors on both sides to borrow their security system SD cards. I was driving them back to the station for viewing when I received your call about Julie's missing status."

"So, you haven't viewed the footage?" Gwen asked.

"I have now," he updated. "First thing this morning."

Ursula jumped to her feet. "And???"

Hc reached over and gently urged her down onto her chair before continuing. "Both cameras were wide angle and included Julie's platform. It appears that Sylvia was arguing with Julie, poking her in the chest. Then Sylvia's hands flew to her own chest, and she stumbled. Zooming in, it's clear that Julie tried to prevent Sylvia from tumbling down those steps to the beach but lost her grip on Sylvia's wet clothing."

Ursula sighed. "Then why did Julie continually claim she wasn't involved?"

Gwen said, "If I recall, she kept saying that she shouldn't be blamed for Sylvia's death."

"You're right," Ursula agreed, then switched her focus back to Ben. "What happens now?"

"Detective Ferguson will turn over both recordings to the DA for analysis."

"And once they watch it, Julie will be released?"

Ben focused on Ursula. "I don't know. Keep in mind she was also charged with failure to report the accident."

Ursula again got to her feet and paced the dining room.

Ben asked her, "Did you catch up with your defense attorney friend?"

"I did. He'll be arriving on the ten o'clock ferry."

Ben turned to Gwen and Tess. "Detective Ferguson officially ended my temporary assignment. If Julie goes to trial... and I'm not at all sure the case will go that far... I might need to come back and testify."

In the recesses of his mind, Ben filed a note that if he did return to Nantucket, he'd invite Gwen to come with him.

"For now," he continued, glancing around the table, "I'm free to leave so I booked my return on that ten o'clock ferry."

When Gwen again looked into Ben's eyes, he couldn't decide how to read her expression. Did she regret he was leaving or was she glad for a break from his unspoken pressure for a more intimate relationship? She was, after all, the one who suggested they delay their discussion until they were both back in Harbor Falls.

Ursula took a position behind her chair, looking first at Tess and then Gwen. "Thank you both for staying to support Julie and me, too. But if you want to ride the ferry back to the mainland with Ben, I won't discourage you."

"I hate to leave you to deal with Julie's arrest by yourself," Tess said.

"I'll be fine," Ursula assured her. "My defense attorney friend will be here with me."

Tess glanced at Gwen. "If you want to go back on the ten o'clock ferry, I'll check if I can rebook our tickets."

Ben held his half-eaten muffin in mid-air. "Most people are traveling *to* Nantucket on Fridays, not *leaving* it."

Gwen tilted her head toward Tess. "One of my students was rescheduled for tomorrow morning, so riding the ferry today would be perfect."

"Then it's settled," Tess said. "I'll call now."

***

Because Ursula promised to retrieve her lawyer friend at the dock, she invited Tess to ride with her.

Gwen wen rode with Ben in his police loaner.

As they both zoomed along the road toward the docks, he reached over and squeezed her hand. "Harbor Falls will be a welcome break after our investigation out here."

Glancing over, she noted his half smile and the twinkle in his grey eyes, almost dreading their upcoming conversation about their conflicting ideas for their personal future.

Gently pulling her hand from under his to search for nothing in her hobo bag, she spoke to Ben sideways. "I can't wait to walk in my front door this afternoon."

258

Minutes later, reaching the dock area, Ursula veered left toward the short-term parking lot across the street from the ferry landing.

Ben parked behind a police cruiser.

Unbuckling and getting out, Gwen stood quietly as Ben chatted with Logan and another patrolman assigned to drive Ben's loaner back to the station.

Logan extended his hand to Ben. "Detective Ferguson is reassigning me to his detective squad."

"Well deserved, Logan. Thanks for your help during the Sylvia Pierce investigation."

"Maybe I'll see you again someday, Ben." Logan returned to his cruiser, the other officer dropped into Ben's loaner, and the two official vehicles drove away.

Gwen hugged Ursula goodbye. Tess did the same, but Ben simply shook Ursula's hand, adding words of encouragement about Julie's situation.

Luggage in hand, Gwen, Ben, and Tess quick-walked toward the boarding queue. Gwen glanced over her shoulder to see Ursula greeting a man in a business suit.

Though the security videos from neighbors might offset the charge of involuntary manslaughter, the remaining charge of failure to report an accident needed to be resolved. How would Julie serve that sentence?

***

As the ferry navigated smoothly across Nantucket Sound, Gwen tapped Tess's arm. "Do you want something to drink?"

259

"Thanks, but no, you and Ben go ahead."

Understanding Tess's concern for her college roommate's legal plight, Gwen signaled Ben to follow her.

In the ferry's snack bar, they ordered hot cider then sat opposite each other in a nearby booth.

Ben rested his forearms on the table and leaned toward her. "Are you okay, Gwen?"

Gwen took another sip. "I'm fine, but I'm worried about Tess. She's agonizing about Julie."

Ben sat back, his expression thoughtful. "If Ursula's lawyer is any good, he'll be able to reduce the severity of the charges."

Avoiding Ben's eyes, Gwen stared out the window, watching the seagulls who flitted alongside the ferry, hoping for a toss of food from a passenger. Swallowing the last of her cider, she slid out of the booth. "I'm going to bring Tess a cup of hot chocolate."

Ben snickered. "Because chocolate in any form can fix just about anything?"

Gwen grinned at him. "Absolutely,"

Returning to their original table on the upper deck, Gwen extended the drink to her sister, who hadn't budged.

Tess accepted the cup, saying only, "Thanks."

When Ben signaled he was going outside to the forward deck, Gwen sat across from her sister and reached for her hand. "Instead of rushing back to the Berkshires, Tess, why don't you stay with me for a few days? There are several autumn craft fairs in Harbor Falls this weekend that we could explore."

"Let me think about that." Tess stared at the shallow white caps tumbling into the waters of Nantucket Sound.

Following Tess's unspoken request to sit in silence, Gwen's mind returned to her plight with Ben.

Inwardly, she cringed. How could she discourage Ben's romantic plans without losing his friendship? Would he accept her resolute faithfulness to Parker based on his promise of their reunion in the afterlife?

And then she remembered her recent disappointment when Parker's spirit hadn't appeared during Sunday's séance. As she had then, Gwen wondered if her link to him had been broken. Or was his appearance blocked by the waters of the Nantucket Sound as Ursula had suggested.

If their link had been broken, would Parker's spirit still be waiting for her?

Gwen racked her brain to think of even one person in her circle of acquaintances who had any hope of answering these questions. No one's name surfaced.

And then a strategy began to form. If Tess stayed for a few days, the idea would have to wait until her sister returned to the Berkshires. Then Gwen would be uninterrupted as she repeated her attempt to connect with Parker's ghost. And then she'd get together with Ben to discourage his plans for romance.

While Tess napped fitfully in the gentle roll of the ferry, Gwen quietly contemplated her plan of action.

First, she'd wander both upstairs and down inside their library home calling Parker's name.

Then she'd relocate to various areas outside in the gardens.

If he didn't respond in either place, she'd drive again to their gravesite in the memorial park.

And finally, the B&B where he'd followed her the year before. The owners would totally understand her intention because of Theo, their inherited ghost.

Gwen would give Parker every chance to hear her voice and come to her. She could only hope her fear of their broken link would be eliminated by his appearance.

Finally glancing out the ferry's window, she noticed the mainland taking shape in the distance. With little choppiness during the cruise to Hyannis, the ferry pulled into the dock a few minutes ahead of the scheduled time.

As Ben rejoined them, Gwen woke Tess with a gentle hand.

The three made their way down the ramp, soon retrieving their luggage from the racks and climbing aboard the courtesy shuttle for the short ride to the remote parking lot.

Tess's hybrid and Ben's corvette were parked side by side.

Ben insisted on lifting their luggage into the back seat, saying, "I'll call you later to be sure you two arrived in Harbor Falls without incident."

"Thanks, Ben," she said. "And let us know if you receive any updates about Julie."

"I'll do that." Ben dropped into his leather driver's seat, waving as he zoomed away.

Gwen watched him disappear from view. After their talk, would he disappear from her life?

Chapter Forty-Two

... mid-day, Friday

As Tess's hybrid circled Library Lane, Gwen's heart warmed at the welcoming sight of her home.

Removing her luggage from Tess's back seat, she noted her sister's solemn expression, a reminder that their journey to Nantucket had gone so sadly wrong. "Will you stay for a few days, Tess? You're too distracted by Julie's situation for the solo drive to the Berkshires this afternoon."

Tess closed the hybrid's door. "I'll at least have a cup of tea with you. Beyond that, I haven't made up my mind."

When they stepped into the foyer, the sound of an insistent meow echoed throughout the open floorplan. Gwen smiled, watching Amber descend the split staircase with regal indifference, as if her mistress had simply returned from grocery shopping rather than being gone for a week.

The feisty feline slithered around Gwen's ankles, then flipped her tail and quick-walked toward the kitchen, glancing over her shoulder to be sure Gwen was following.

Nudging Tess, Gwen snickered. "See how much Amber missed me? She only wants to be fed. She was well-tended by both Liz and Jenna, but Amber will pester me until I fill her bowls. It's a wonder she's not chunkier."

Mere seconds after a token nibble and a lap of fresh water, the cat allowed Gwen to pat her golden head before scooting up the staircase toward the mezzanine.

Sighing with satisfaction to be home, Gwen filled the teakettle and placed it on the stove to boil.

Tess's cell buzzed.

Gwen's doorbell chimed.

Opening the heavy oak door, she found Ben sliding his cell phone into his jacket pocket. "I've got news about Julie from Detective Ferguson."

Gwen waved him inside and they both nearly crashed into Tess who was rushing toward them, speaking into her own cell phone, "That's such a relief. Thanks for calling."

"Did we receive the same news?" Ben asked, looking from one sister to the other.

Tess beamed. "An update from Ursula."

When the kettle began to whistle, Gwen urged them toward the kitchen. "Hold your news until I set our tea to steep."

In less than a minute, Gwen placed three mugs of Earl Grey on the island counter. "Now you can share your news."

"Ladies first." Ben's gaze focused on Tess.

Words tumbled out. "By the time Ursula brought her lawyer friend to the police station, the final coroner's report had arrived. Sylvia died of a heart attack. Falling down those steps was not the cause of her death."

Gwen glanced at Ben. "Does that match what Detective Ferguson told you?"

Ben dunked his tea bag and nodded. "It does, plus a bit more detail. Everyone mistakenly assumed that Sylvia drowned because her body was tangled in the bottom railings at the beach. But her lungs didn't contain salty ocean water, which confirms she wasn't breathing when the storm surge reached her."

Gwen stirred raw sugar into her Earl Grey. "That also explains why no storm watchers heard her scream. She didn't scream because she had already died."

Her smile wide, Tess added, "Ursula's lawyer friend argued that based on the coroner's report plus the video showing Julie losing her grip on Sylvia's clothing, Julie cannot be blamed for Sylvia's tragic death."

"Exactly," Ben confirmed. "The involuntary manslaughter charge has been dropped. Though Julie still has to face the charge of failure to report an accident."

"What's the punishment for that?" Tess asked.

"Most likely community service," Ben answered.

"Well, here's the best part," Tess went on. "The judge released Julie with strict orders not to leave Nantucket until he rules on that lesser charge. Ursula drove them both home a little while ago. I'm so relieved."

Gwen asked, "Did Ursula say if she asked Julie why she didn't call for help after Sylvia fell down those steps?"

"She did. Julie explained that she panicked. If anyone had seen them together on the platform, it could appear she was pushing Sylvia when she was only trying to keep the woman from falling. She crossed her fingers that Sylvia would survive her slide down to the beach and that her drunken brain might not remember the incident, so Julie decided to say nothing about Sylvia's tumble."

"We can all justify anything," Ben commented.

"At least the fact that Sylvia suffered a heart attack is some small comfort," Gwen added.

The door to the rear deck opened and Jenna rushed into the kitchen. "Welcome back, my sort-of grandmother! I never realized how much I'd miss you."

"I missed you, too, my sort-of granddaughter." Gwen moved away from Tess to exchange hugs with Jenna. Their joshing about their relationship always lightened Gwen's heart and mind.

Releasing Gwen, Jenna made eye contact with Tess, then Ben. "Welcome back to both of you, too."

Tess laughed. "Glad you noticed us." To Gwen, she said, "If your invitation to stay for a few days is still on the table, I accept. I'm in a much brighter mood now."

"Oh, good," Gwen replied, her reaction now mixed.

Though thrilled that Tess wasn't leaving right away, Gwen's search for Parker followed by her conversation with Ben were again put on hold.

***

The lively chatter between Gwen, Jenna, and Tess didn't include Ben, so he said his goodbyes and drove toward his apartment on the outskirts of Harbor Falls.

As the road ribboned behind him in his rearview mirror, a conversation with Julie surfaced in Ben's mind. She'd asked if he believed in ghosts.

He'd avoided a direct answer because he still had a tough time grasping their existence. He'd always assumed ghosts were a figment of the imagination or wishful thinking by a loved one left behind.

That is, until his overwhelming face to face encounter with the ghost inhabiting the Harbor Falls B&B.

Soon afterwards, Gwen confided that her husband's spirit often visited her. Not long after that, she'd introduced him to her Parker's ghost. The transparent spirit had even spoken to Ben, leaving no doubt that Gwen and Parker shared an unusual and extraordinarily strong paranormal bond.

Did that bond explain Gwen's recent coolness? Had Parker discouraged her from encouraging a connection with Ben?

If true, how in the world would he convince her to entertain the idea of a closer relationship?

Because the heartfelt conversation he envisioned required privacy, Ben had no choice but to wait until Gwen's time with Tess and Jenna ended. At the first opportunity, he'd somehow arrange some quiet time with the lady.

His unknown future with Gwen haunted Ben throughout the rest of the day and into the night, interrupting his sleep, and causing unsettling dreams of being alone.

He awoke groggy and heavy-eyed on Saturday morning, forcing himself from his apartment for his morning jog.

Chapter Forty-Three

… mid-morning, the following Monday

After wandering the craft fairs and dining at seashore restaurants, Gwen and Jenna prepared a breakfast of French toast, sausage, and hash brown potatoes as a send-off before Tess drove to her home in the Berkshires.

Waving as Tess's hybrid circled the village green, Jenna murmured, "This weekend with your sister was wonderful, but now I need to finish a paper. Do you mind if I head over to the campus library?"

"Of course not," Gwen said, reaching over to tuck a strand of blonde hair behind her sort-of-granddaughter's ear. "That's the best place to concentrate. See you later."

Entering her foyer, Gwen was nearly overwhelmed by the silence. No Tess. No Jenna. No Amber. She reached for Parker's framed photo, her fingers touching the square lines of his jaw, his mischievous grin. Once again, she wondered why his spirit hadn't materialized during Ursula's second séance in Julie's Nantucket studio.

Were Parker's allotment of earthly visits depleted? Gwen settled in his recliner, calling, "Parker, can you hear me?"

Gazing across the open floor plan, she watched and waited for his translucent self to materialize.

The air around her remained still.

Once again she called his name, and then again, each time more forcefully. Still no glimpse of Parker's spirit.

She wandered into her music studio, then the kitchen, upstairs to the bedrooms and elongated sitting room, and even down into the basement laundry area. No response to her calling Parker's name.

Outside, she moved from one area of the back gardens to another, finally settling on the swing.

Fear cloaked Gwen. Would she ever see Parker again?

At this point, who could say? She doubted that even Ursula could offer any answers.

Once again, Gwen was on her own.

What if her connection with Parker had been irrevocably severed? Would they still reunite in the afterlife? Should she hold tight to her belief that his spirit still waited for her?

And the most dangerous question of all… did she dare consider a romantic entanglement with Ben? Time to explain her complicated plight to the white-haired detective.

Retreating inside, she sat with Parker's beach photo on her lap and dialed Ben's cell. Half-hoping to be sent to his voicemail, she stiffened when he answered on the third ring.

"Hi, Gwen."

"Hi, yourself." Memories of being a tongue-tied teenager emerged as she stumbled for the right words.

Fortunately, Ben filled the gap. "Did you enjoy your weekend with Tess and Jenna?"

Gwen breathed easier. That was one question she could answer. "I did. Tess drove off a few minutes ago."

"Sounds like peace and quiet at your place."

"Jenna's on her way to the college library. The silence is deafening," she quipped. "Has our police chief wrangled you into another investigation yet?"

"I'm not sure he's aware that I'm back from Nantucket, so the answer is no. But if and when he calls, I'll refuse."

"In that case, can I interest you in a cup of coffee?"

"That's right. You bought a replacement carafe."

Though Ben couldn't see her, Gwen grinned. "Yes, I did. Last week after Tess and I shopped for Halloween costumes."

"Well, even if you hadn't bribed me with the best brew in Harbor Falls, we need to talk. Be there soon."

Gwen suddenly regretted inviting him over.

But she'd promised him coffee, so she placed Parker's photo on the island countertop and set the coffee maker to brew, her hands shaking as she reached for two mugs.

The deep rumble of Ben's corvette announced his arrival. Quick walking through the foyer, she swung open the oak door just as his finger stretched toward the doorbell.

His amused expression morphed into concern. "Are you all right, Gwen?"

***

At a loss to understand the change in Gwen's demeanor, Ben guided her to the leather sofa. "You stay here. I'll fetch our coffee."

With two steaming mugs in hand, he extended one toward Gwen as he settled on the adjacent cushion.

"What's wrong? You sounded fine on the phone."

Her eyes moistened. "I don't know where to begin."

"No rush. I'm not leaving any time soon."

She half grinned. "Even if the chief pesters you?"

"Even then."

When she remained silent, Ben said, "How about I talk while you gather your thoughts?"

Gwen's nod was barely discernable.

"First," he began, "Nantucket aside, I apologize again that I've been busy placating our chief since I retired a few months ago and haven't spent much time with you. Starting right now, that is going to change. If you're still interested, that is."

He hesitated. "Do you recall our conversation in the emergency room back in June?"

Her head jerked up. "I was a bit woozy."

"Then I'll refresh your memory. I told you how much I care for you and hinted at a future marriage proposal."

When Gwen didn't react, he forged ahead. "You joked you'd never get married in your jinxed back gardens."

Gwen blurted, "Something else happened earlier that day."

Her words filling him with a sudden chill, Ben stepped to the fireplace. "Okay if I light a fire?"

She nodded her consent, so he arranged a few small logs and minimal kindling, then struck a match to crinkled newspaper. Unsure he wanted to hear what Gwen was about to tell him, he perched on the edge of Parker's recliner and rested his forearms on his knees. "I'm listening."

***

Taken aback by the impatience in Ben's tone, Gwen blew out a lungful of air. Juggling her affection for Ben with her loving loyalty to Parker had become increasingly complicated.

Inhaling once more, Gwen took the plunge. "I know what I'm about to say sounds bizarre. I'm trusting you'll believe me because you've met Parker's ghost."

"That's not an introduction I'm likely to forget. Why are you bringing it up now?"

"Back in June, before you discovered me passed out in Parker's recliner…"

When she pointed to where Ben sat, he jumped up and poked at the low-burning fire, his back to her.

Without commenting on Ben's reaction, she continued. "…and Parker's ghost appeared to me. I floated from my body and reached for his hand, fully expecting to walk into the afterlife with him."

Ben whirled toward her, knelt down, and grasped her hands. "You mean you died? But I don't understand. You're here with me now."

His statement of the obvious hung in the air.

In that instant, Gwen's indecisiveness vanished. Her future with Ben was clear. She would not risk her hopefully untarnished link with Parker's spirit by allowing a physical relationship with Ben… or any earthly man for that matter.

"Yes, Ben, I *am* here now. Parker said it wasn't my time and pushed my spirit back toward my body. Then you and Jenna found me and called the ambulance."

Ben sat in silence.

Gwen dared to continue. "Parker's spirit promised he'll be waiting for me. Then I woke up in the emergency room. And Ben, I *do* remember our hospital conversation."

A ray of hope brightened his eyes.

"I'm sorry my careless words misled you. My attempt at humor didn't mean I'd accept your marriage proposal."

"If I ever actually proposed, you mean?"

She focused first on Ben's left eye, then on his right, and back again. "You can joke all you want, but I came this close to walking into the afterlife with my Parker." She closed her thumb and first finger until they nearly touched to visually illustrate her point.

And then she added, "I don't know if my interim link with Parker has been severed, but I honestly believe he'll be waiting for me when my final day on earth arrives. That's why I've been resisting your romantic advances. Marrying again could destroy my reunion with Parker in the afterlife, and I'm sorry, Ben, but I'm not willing to take that risk."

Chapter Forty-Four

… late-morning, Monday

For a full minute, Ben couldn't speak until he said, "This is not at all what I expected you to tell me, but it explains your recent coolness. Most widows marry again."

"That may be true for some, Ben. I'm so sorry if you were planning for us to walk down the aisle one day."

"My logical brain understands your devotion to Parker. If all widows communicated with their first husband's spirit like you have, Gwen, they might not remarry either."

The pain of her rejection roiling Ben's stomach, he wandered to the fireplace and poked at the low flames.

His new expectation coming into focus, Ben whirled to face her. "I don't want to sacrifice our friendship, Gwen, because no one else can take your place at this stage of my life. Can we at least remain friends? Strictly platonic friends?"

A big smile lit up her face.

"I see you're pleased." Ben joined her on the sofa and touched the knuckles of her closest hand. "Do you mind?"

When she wiggled her fingers, Ben squeezed gently and said, "I've missed our dinners and back road adventures."

She reached over and enclosed his free hand. "Me, too. Can I interest you in Thanksgiving dinner at Tess's?"

"Thanksgiving in the Berkshires? I accept."

***

Knowing Ben wouldn't object to a harmless show of affection between friends, Gwen drew him into her arms and held on tight.

"Thanksgiving is weeks away," he murmured into her ear. "How about something for right now?"

Disengaging from her embrace, Ben got to his feet, regripped her hand and guided her to the front window.

He waved toward his red Corvette gleaming at the curb. "The sun is shining and there's an autumn chill in the air. Perfect weather for a drive. You game, Gwen?"

Relieved that her devotion to Parker remained intact and her friendship with Ben would continue, Gwen aimed a happy grin his way.

"I can think of nothing I'd rather do, Ben. But first, let's separate those small logs and close the glass screen to dampen the fire. Then let's get out of here before the chief finds out you're back in Harbor Falls."

THE END